CONSTABLE GOES TO MARKET

Normally quiet and peaceful, Ashfordly comes alive with traders and customers on market day – and such gatherings are never without problems for Constable Nick. He copes with a wandering flock of geese on the village green and deals with near disaster when Greengrass's dog, Alfred, demolishes market stalls in his quest to catch a white rabbit. And how did a live hand grenade come to be left among the potatoes? There are linguistic misunderstandings, people behaving with typical British stupidity and even a crime or two – it's all in a day's work for Constable Nick of Aidensfield.

CONSTABLE GOES
TO MARKET

Constable Goes To Market

by

Nicholas Rhea

Magna Large Print Books
Long Preston, North Yorkshire,
BD23 4ND, England.

British Library Cataloguing in Publication Data.

Rhea, Nicholas
    Constable goes to market.

    A catalogue record of this book is
    available from the British Library

    ISBN   0-7505-1898-7

First published in Great Britain in 2002 by Robert Hale Limited

Copyright © Nicholas Rhea 2002

Cover illustration © Barbara Walton by arrangement with
Robert Hale Ltd.

Published in Large Print 2002 by arrangement with
Robert Hale Limited

Magna Large Print is an imprint of Library Magna Books Ltd.

Printed and bound in Great Britain by
T.J. (International) Ltd., Cornwall, PL28 8RW

00363101

Chapter One

Ashfordly was one of many small but thriving market-towns in the North Riding of Yorkshire. Taking them as a whole, it was possible to visit a produce market somewhere in the county every day of the week except Sunday. In some cases, two or more markets were held the same day in separate parts of the county, while some towns managed to support two markets in a single week – and one or two of those even held cattle marts as well. For example, Thirsk, Whitby and Pickering markets were on Monday; Hawes and Bedale on Tuesday; Masham, Kirkbymoorside, Whitby and Northallerton on Wednesday; Scarborough and Guisborough on Thursday, with Easingwold, Helmsley, Stokesley and Leyburn each Friday. On Saturday there were markets in Malton, Richmond, Guisborough, Thirsk and Northallerton.

When I was the constable at Aidensfield, Guisborough was within the North Riding of Yorkshire but along with a large tract of land and many other towns like Yarm, Saltburn, Redcar, Thornaby, Middlesbrough and Loftus, it was transferred to newly formed Cleveland County on 1 April, 1974. If we lost that slice of our former county, however, we gained from the West Riding some equally splendid market-towns, including Ripon, Ingleton, Knaresborough, Selby, Settle, Skipton and Tadcaster. These historic gains and losses helped to create a brand new county called North Yorkshire, of which Harrogate and York also became a part.

Geographically, North Yorkshire became England's largest county – and that was without West Yorkshire, South Yorkshire and the East Riding which became part of Humberside.

Despite York's famous, imposing and historic presence, however, Northallerton, the former county town of the North Riding, became North Yorkshire's county town and headquarters of the county council, police authority, fire authority and other institutions. But none of those changes had occurred as I patrolled my patch at Aidensield – at that time, I was still a member of the North Riding of Yorkshire Constabulary, not the North Yorkshire Police!

So far as markets were concerned, Ashfordly's was every Friday except for Good Friday or when Christmas Day fell on a Friday. Although the event required very little police attention, it was never dull or quiet; rather, it was enjoyable, invariably stimulating and always interesting. A thriving produce market had been a feature of Ashfordly's ancient square since being established by charter in 1329 during the reign of Edward III. From then on down the centuries, country people from the surrounding villages had made their way to market without interruption – the market had even continued throughout the two World Wars – and there is little doubt that this outlet enabled many to earn a reasonable living from the land.

The act of buying and selling, with the inevitable bartering and bargaining, provided a wonderful sense of everlasting history and perpetuated a colourful way of life which has changed very little down the centuries.

In addition, of course, a trip to market was a good excuse for socializing – especially as the inns surrounding the market-place were open all day thanks to a very popular legal device known officially as a General Order of Exemption, but less formally as the market-day extension. This allowed people to drink alcohol in selected pubs from opening-time in the morning without a break until closing-time in the evening. This was a treat not available on other days or in non-market-towns and there is little doubt this extension of drinking hours encouraged people to visit the town every Friday. Some busy-bodies, probably with nothing better to do, queried whether such visitors were *bona fide* market-traders or some other person whose attendance at the market was essential. But that was not the issue. The fact was that Ashfordly's weekly market qualified selected inns to benefit from that relaxation of the liquor licensing laws.

Ashfordly's market-square occupied a strategic position in the very centre of the town. It was the focal point for a range of activities and was a large cobbled area surrounded by colourful shops, inns and private houses. There was also a stone-built town hall and former police station, later turned into a café; these dominated the western edge of the market-square. On the northern boundary was the half-timbered Swan Hotel – only yards away from the King's Head, with sundry banks, cafés, inns, shops and private houses beneath an undulating tumble of roofs forming the remaining sides of the square. Well maintained with troughs of flowers around its extremities, the square was owned by Ashfordly Estate and served as a free car-park during the week.

There was ample car-parking space here without any limit on the duration of a stay, a boon to tourists, shoppers and overnight visitors – and thus a great benefit to the business life of the town.

Dominating the square was a huge stone memorial to Harold, the third Baron Ashfordly, a gift from his family, friends and staff, while in the north-western corner was the scant remains of the former market-cross. At one time, the formal start to the weekly market was heralded by a bell being rung at this cross, but that custom had ended long ago. There had often been suggestions that the cross be restored, but during my time as the village constable at Aidensfield, no plans ever came to fruition.

Hidden behind the town hall, and often ignored by visitors, was Ashfordly Castle, and although this was not in the major league, like Richmond Castle, or even Pickering, in terms of historic note and dramatic impact, it was nonetheless very interesting and worth a visit. Also tucked behind some towering trees to the north of the square was the impressive parish church of All Saints with its tower and noisy clock which struck every quarter of an hour, day and night, much to the consternation of sleepy visitors in the nearby hotels. For the lonely constable patrolling those quiet streets at night, however, the presence of that clock with its repetitive strikes was most reassuring.

During the daytime hours each week, the market-square was quiet with pensioners sitting on seats and doing little but chat and reminisce. Tourists took photographs and cyclists wondered where to park their precious machines.

Ladies met one another beneath the Ashfordly Memorial before heading off to the shops or opting for a quiet lunch or relaxing coffee, and a lot of working men found time to linger until the opening of the pubs. Every Friday, however, parking by the public was forbidden upon most of the cobbles on the square and, from around 4.30 a.m., even in the darkness of winter, the square rapidly filled with rows of stalls with colourful canvas roofs, all overflowing with wonderful things – fresh fruit and vegetables, fish, clothes, shoes and hats, kitchen utensils and furniture polish, homemade cakes and bread, sweets, cheese, eggs and butter, toys and handicrafts of various kinds, antiques, bric-a-brac and even fittings for motor cars like wing mirrors, seat covers and badges. The whole place was transformed into a noisy, happy scene with the sounds of music from some stalls, purveyors shouting their wares from others and people gossiping, exchanging trade news, meeting old friends while all the time conducting the age-old practice of buying and selling.

This was not a livestock mart, however. The nearest cattle mart was held at Brantsford on Wednesdays and, in spite of its name suggesting it traded only in cattle, it included pigs, sheep and goats. In fact, some stalls sold smaller animals – Claude Jeremiah Greengrass often turned up with day-old chicks and goslings. Puppies and kittens were sold too and one could almost guarantee a stall which offered guinea pigs, newts and snakes, as well as goldfish in jam-jars and later in plastic bags. Sometimes, the definition of 'livestock' so far as market-trading was concerned, raised interesting questions – was a trader selling maggots to anglers, trading in livestock?

At a superficial level, there seems nothing in this very English way of life that might concern the police, but for every market-day in Ashfordly, one of the local constables was detailed for market duties. Generally, the task fell to one of the constables stationed at Ashfordly, but occasionally, one of the bobbies from the surrounding villages was detailed. My turn came periodically and I had also to attend, on occasions, one of the local cattle marts, chiefly to issue livestock movement licences, but there were no such formal duties at the weekly produce markets. It was usually a case of patrolling the market in uniform to deal with anything that might arise and at the same time keeping an eye open for minor forms of law-breaking. Occasionally, we received reports of thefts from market-stalls or even instances of pick-pocketing, but complaints about the sale of inferior goods was seldom a matter for the police unless they involved some blatant fraud or false pretences. Those who complained about the quality of goods were referred to the relevant department of the local authority. In addition, there was always the likelihood that stolen goods might be sold by less-than-honest market-traders, this being an ideal means of disposing of illicitly obtained goods.

If there was likely to be trouble or a problem of any kind, it usually arose from drivers causing obstruction by parking their vehicles in silly places, or revellers drinking rather too much alcohol, not surprising given the fact they had all day to do so and that a good day's trading was usually an excuse for a celebration. On occasions, this did result in rather high spirits.

Fights could break out, sometimes with ensuing arrests of the participants for either being drunk and incapable or drunk and disorderly. Sometimes, they were charged with one of the public order offences if their conduct justified it.

As one of the village constables for whom Ashfordly Police Station was the Section Office, and with Sergeant Craddock in charge of allocating our duties, I had to take my turn patrolling Ashfordly on market-day. This might be a four-hour spell incorporating the market as well as other parts of the small town, or it might be a full eight-hour tour of duty in the town, but always with the market as the focal point on Fridays. I must admit I enjoyed market-day duties for they were invariably a genuine pleasure, as was the banter and cheerful atmosphere. The hustle and bustle of the passing scene was a pleasant contrast to the solitude of Aidensfield, and the opportunity to walk among the public as they inspected, considered and discussed the goods on offer was a tonic.

Even though complaints and reports of trouble were rare, I was once faced with a very baffling problem. I was on duty in uniform and patrolling among the market stalls when the cheeseman said he'd like a quiet word with me. He and his wife ran a very popular stall which offered a very wide range of cheeses; they sold everything; from Wensleydale to Stilton by way of Edam and goats' cheese from Greece, and claimed they could supply every known British cheese. Mary and I would often buy our supplies from this stall, and a lot of the inns and hotels in Ashfordly did likewise.

The cheeseman was called Tony Lofthouse and his home was at Driffield in East Yorkshire; he and his wife, Lena, attended several markets in the North Riding as well as some in the East Riding. In their late forties, they were a very pleasant couple, with the bespectacled Tony, only some five feet two inches tall, having a head of thick

16

silver hair which made him look older than his years. Lena, a tiny woman with twinkling eyes and a rich head of warm brown hair, was always cheerful and anxious to please her many customers. It was while I was passing through one of the thronged avenues created by several busy stalls that Tony hailed me.

'Can I have a word, PC Rhea?'

'Of course,' I responded.

'I don't want to be a nuisance, or sound as if I am a troublemaker, but did you see that cheese stall on the Brantsford road this morning?'

I shook my head. 'No, Tony, I don't come to Ashfordly that way, I always come from Aidensfield via Briggsby. Why? Is there a problem?'

'Well, yes, he's been there four or five times now, and this morning I happened to see one of my regular customers buying from him, instead of coming here to get supplies from me.'

'Sneaky!' I said.

'Very, and unfair.' Tony was not at all amused by this competitor's activities. 'He seems to be setting himself up on Fridays deliberately to attract people heading to market, and then selling cheeses to them

17

before they get here. His prices are a bit cheaper than mine, too; he's undercutting me, Mr Rhea; he's harming my business.'

'Unfair competition?' I suggested.

'Very!' he emphasized. 'And it's affecting my turnover. Over the past week or two, I've noticed some of my former regulars aren't coming any more, they're getting their stuff from him.'

'Unfortunate though it is, Tony, I feel this is hardly a matter for the police,' I began.

'Isn't it? I thought it was a criminal offence,' he put to me.

'If it is, I've never heard about it, but I'll make enquiries.' I was baffled by Tony's assertion that this could be a criminal matter. I thought I was *au fait* with most aspects of criminal law, but I'd never known this kind of activity be within the scope of criminal law or police work.

'It's right enough, I read it somewhere,' Tony assured me. 'In one of our trade journals, I think.'

'Right. So who is this man?' I asked, never having seen him in action.

'He's operating from a small cottage right on the corner where the road from Stovensby rises to the junction with the Brantsford-Ashfordly road,' he said. 'It was sold a few

18

months ago; this chap is the new owner I think. I've no idea what he's called or where he's come from. All I know is that when I'm heading for Ashfordly market, there's a stall outside his cottage offering cheeses for sale, all kinds of cheeses. He's not often standing at his stall – there's price labels stuck into every one and you knock on the door to pay. He's been doing it for four or five weeks now.'

By quizzing Tony, the only information I could glean was that he had read in some magazine or periodical that people who sold goods along the route to a market were breaking the law and could be prosecuted. He had no wish to be vindictive although he did wish to protect his own business. If the fellow was breaking the law, then Tony felt he should be warned of his transgression. Stopping him would be preferable to a prosecution in court; a warning should be sufficient.

'I'm not sure he is breaking any criminal law,' I had to tell Tony. 'I know of no law which forbids him to sell goods out of town on the day of a market.'

'There is, Mr Rhea, I'm sure of it. It's all to do with fair trading and reasonable competition in the market-place.'

19

'Can you find the reference for me?' I put to him. 'Either give me a ring or let me know next time you are here.'

'I might have thrown it out but I'll check when I get home.'

'Thanks. If it's some new statute of a very specialized nature, we might not have been made aware of it. In the meantime, I'll make my own enquiries and if that man is breaking the criminal law, I'll submit a report to my superiors. Is he obstructing the highway with his stall, or is traffic causing a problem by halting there?'

'Oh, no, nothing like that. There's a substantial lay-by; he's not creating any kind of traffic hazard. I don't want to be vindictive, as I said, and I do think I can undercut him... I've seen his prices and mine are cheaper today ... but he's catching his customers by unfair means and it doesn't help if my profits are down.'

'I can't consider the loss or profit motive,' I smiled. 'I'm only concerned with law-breaking.'

'I appreciate that, but I've still got my expenses to meet – and he is breaking the law, that's why I'm reporting it to you.'

I knew the cottage in question, although I didn't know its name or the name of any new occupant or owner, but I assured Tony I would do my best to deal with his problem. At the same time, I had to be very cautious in my approach to this because I must not get involved in disputes which were of a private nature, or those for which a civil remedy was required, rather than interference by the police. I could not be sure that this problem was in breach of any criminal law but if there was any kind of law-breaking, I felt sure it would infringe the regulations which governed the sale of food. Those were not normally within the scope of police duty, but Tony's insistence that the criminal law was being broken meant I had to investigate the matter. I decided to examine all the laws on market-trading before interviewing the rogue cheese seller. I realized, also, that I would have to inform Sergeant Craddock of this development. After explaining my caution to Tony, I continued my patrol without further incident and it was later that day when Sergeant Craddock met me at a rendezvous point.

'Anything to report, PC Rhea?' he asked.

I told him about the complaint from Tony Lofthouse and his reaction was entirely predictable.

21

'That is most definitely not a police matter, PC Rhea, such goings-on are not breaches of criminal law. If your Mr Lofthouse has a grievance about a competitor's behaviour, or an alleged breach of regulations, he should get in touch with the local authority: they administer the laws governing the sale of food and drugs. There might be some breach of the Food and Drugs Act of 1955, PC Rhea. So that's your course of action – get him to ring County Hall at Northallerton and ask to speak to a food inspector. Apart from anything else, there may be breaches of the hygiene regulations. But it is not for us to investigate this complaint.'

'Right, Sergeant.'

In spite of Craddock's stout denial of the need for police involvement, I was still puzzled by Tony Lofthouse's insistence that his competitor was breaching criminal law. He was adamant he'd read it in some journal or other, so I decided to examine my law books when I returned home. I discovered some interesting snippets about markets – for example, in the past these were held on Sundays and holy days of obligation (later known as holidays) When England was a Catholic country, the faithful attended mass on Sundays and holy days. At that time, markets were always close to a church so that the congregation could visit the market while fulfilling their religious duties. When some enterprising market-traders felt it a good idea to establish their stalls in the churchyard, however, this development was quickly forbidden. The noise and disturbance was too much and so, in 1285, Edward I made it illegal to hold markets in churchyards.

In 1448, Sunday markets were forbidden too, except on four Sundays during harvest time, but by 1677 Charles II had decreed that markets were illegal on any Sunday.

I came across some very ancient laws, one of which said that one market should be distant from another (was a single stall outside a house classed as a market? I asked myself), while another said that if a man erected a market-stall too close to another selling the same sort of goods, a legal action might follow. Likewise, I learned that a butcher must not sell meat from his house on market-day – it had to be sold in the open market, and the market should also be equipped with pillories and tumbrels to punish offenders. There were rules about paying tolls, not selling after sunset or before sunrise, allowing strangers the right to purchase goods, making sure there was sufficient space for people to pass and repass between the stalls and, most important, that any sale must be in the open so that anyone passing by was able to see it available for purchase. The whole idea of a market was that goods must be freely displayed and that competitive prices prevailed. Fraudulent sales were illegal as was the sale of stolen property, but the overriding theme, constantly reiterated, was that any sale must be in the open market so that fairness and competition in prices were honoured. But all these rules dated to around 1754. From my point of view, they were about two centuries out of date, but it seemed to me that the essential thing about those old laws was that they stressed the all-important aspect of goods being sold on the open market. It had to be a market that was available to all, stranger and resident alike, so that genuine competition and fair prices were achieved.

I began to wonder if Tony Lofthouse had come across a statute of similar age, or perhaps misunderstood something he had read. And then I found what I sought. It was an ancient offence known as forestalling, committed by people known as forestallers. Associated offences were committed by regrators and engrossers. These offences were all linked to the essential rule that the market must be open to all and there were very stringent rules against anyone buying livestock, meat, corn, dairy products or any other provisions *before* they reached market and before the bell rang to announce the official opening of the market. Anyone caught forestalling, engrossing or regratoring was severely punished.

So far as forestalling was concerned, there was nothing to prevent anyone buying livestock, dairy products etc direct from a farmer, but it was illegal to meet anyone heading for market to sell their livestock, dairy produce, corn, etc, and then to buy those items before they could be sold on the open market. Forestalling – i.e. buying goods which were on their way to market – was regarded as a serious offence against public trade for it avoided their sale in the face of fair competition. I think this is what Tony had read – except that in his case, the cheeses themselves were not *en route* to market, even if the people who bought them were!

Engrossers bought up large quantities of

goods before those goods reached market – the buyers could then impose their own uncompetitive prices when they re-sold them. Regrators bought goods *en route* to a market and sold them at the same market, or within four miles of it, thus inflating the prices and not allowing the goods to be sold openly with fair competition.

The laws against forestalling, regratoring and engrossing came into being between the reins of Edward I and III but they were abolished during the early years of the reign of George III (1738-1820). From my own researches, I could happily tell Tony Lofthouse that the law he had read had been repealed some two centuries earlier. I decided not to tell Sergeant Craddock of my discoveries, but after explaining things to Tony and receiving his confirmation that this was what he had read in some obscure magazine without realizing it was now repealed legislation, I suggested he'd have to find some other more modern way of coping with his troublesome cheese competitor. I suggested the food hygiene regulations might provide a good starting point, stressing that such a matter was not within the scope of police duties. Had it not been for King George III's legislators,

forestalling might have been part of my
police work and at least I had learned the
origins of that word.

Chapter Two

My periodic duties at Ashfordly market were sufficient for me to realize that certain people could be classed as regular attenders. Each week, they travelled into town from the surrounding villages to spend time at the market, meeting friends, completing some necessary shopping, visiting the bank, their accountant or perhaps the dentist, or merely pottering among the stalls to enjoy the prevailing atmosphere. For some, it was a weekly treat and a welcome break in their domestic routine. Oddly enough, although this was not a cattle or livestock mart, I began to realize that many of the so-called regulars were farmers or farmers' wives. I think they regarded this as a day off work because attendance at the cattle mart would be regarded as part of their business life and, of course, they also worked every weekend. So they considered Friday at the market as a day out, a brief holiday for both man and wife. Many would meet in the hotels, restaurants and pubs, where the men enjoyed a hefty lunch over a few pints of best bitter and the ladies settled for something more genteel, aided by gin and tonic. In spite of the leisurely nature of these outings, there is little doubt that they encompassed a considerable amount of business like wheeling and dealing.

It seemed inevitable that the men would become separated from the women – each had their own things to do. The women met and talked about families and female things while their menfolk did whatever they had to do on such a day. Over the years, a pattern of behaviour had developed because, for most farmers, the reality was that they had no real day off work.

Farming is a complete way of life, not merely a job or profession, so a good deal of useful business, by both men and women, was conducted in and around Ashfordly market during those so-called leisure moments.

Over the weeks, I noticed that a group of young men came to Ashfordly market every Friday, and they always disappeared into the bar of the King's Head for lunch. There would be more than a dozen of them – fifteen or so as a rule – and all were in their mid-twenties or early thirties. They arrived either by car or motor cycle, sometimes sharing transport, although one or two were known to travel by tractor or even cattle truck. Their mode of dress – sturdy workaday clothing – told me they were from an agricultural background, and in time, I began to recognize one or two of them as the sons of local farmers. They had money, that was evident from their demeanour and conduct, so they were not farm labourers, but rather they were lads from well established farming backgrounds. This weekly gathering appeared to be their day off – like all farmers, I knew they would have to work at weekends because they were not employees as such and most of these lads would probably be partners in their family business, destined to inherit their parents' properties in due course.

With such a group of fit and boisterous young men meeting regularly for several pints of beer fortified with something like steak pie and chips, it is not surprising that we, as police officers, wondered when trouble was going to erupt, and what form it would take. The lads were noisy and fun-loving, and the more they consumed, the more relaxed and vociferous they became.

I knew of their whereabouts chiefly

because of the noise, and there is little doubt their presence persuaded others not to venture into that warm and welcoming bar. Quite simply, other visitors could not be heard above the din, and the bawdy sense of humour which accompanied that din was not to everyone's taste. In spite of this, they never got drunk and trouble never erupted – all that happened was a lot of noise comprising mainly loud chatter and raucous laughter.

One of my police duties was to visit pubs during licensing hours to ensure there was no law-breaking or trouble, a task which was welcomed by most landlords, especially towards the end of a busy market-day. During each market-day, therefore, every bobby who patrolled Ashfordly made a point of popping into the bar of the King's Head when these lads were present. The visits were designed to make the lads aware of our presence in the hope it would dissuade them from causing undue annoyance, and the sight of our uniforms invariably provoked a loud cheer and some humorous comments, but it was all done without malice and mischief. In spite of their noise and banter, there was never any question of loutish or malevolent behaviour among those lads, none of them was ever found over the drink-driving limit (those who drove themselves to town always took great care not to drink too much). They never caused trouble either in the pub or in the town, and I later discovered they always donated their small change to local charities following those lunches, popping their coins into collection boxes on the bar counter. What emerged was that they were a bunch of very likeable and jolly young men.

Eventually, once he realised the group had become a permanent fixture during his Friday lunchtime, the landlord of the King's Head, Jim Woodruff, decided they would be best catered for if they used a private room for their meetings. As regular customers, their presence was important to the inn's business and if Jim persuaded them to use a separate room, it would free that corner of the bar for other customers – and it would considerably reduce the noise levels! Jim had several small rooms on the ground floor and he decided to place them in the Castle Room, a very comfortable place often used for small conferences. The lads were delighted and promptly named themselves the Castle Club, later producing a T-shirt bearing that name and a logo of Ashfordly

Castle, both of which were utilized in raising funds for a host of local charities.

My visits to the Castle Room were not very frequent, but we had to show the uniform during official visits to the pub and so it was, due to those spasmodic visits over the months, I noticed that one of the lads never had a pint of beer in front of him. His pint glass always seemed to contain squash, and I assumed it was because he was driving some of the others home. Quietly, I admired the lad for his wisdom, but on another occasion one evening I saw him in a different pub, this time with a pretty girl, and again his drink was orange juice. Although this seemed odd in a sturdy, handsome and well-to-do young man, I thought perhaps he might have a medical condition which demanded abstention from alcohol, or, of course, he might be ultra-careful so far as his driving was concerned, or he might avoid alcohol for religious reasons.

But it was nothing to do with me – what he drank was of no concern, but I thought it odd that a lad who never drank beer seemed more than happy to resort to public houses with a crowd of people who drank profusely. Usually, non-drinkers kept well clear of places which dispensed the demon drink (and the people who drank it) just in case the temptation was too much to bear.

Then, one evening at closing-time, I popped into the Brewers Arms at Aidensfield. I was on duty and this was one of my routine pub visits; the place was fairly quiet and most of the people were leaving as I entered. As I made for the bar, I saw the orange-drinking lad and his girlfriend – they were just leaving too, and he bade me good-night while she produced a lovely smile. In a minute or two, the place was empty.

'Was it something I said, or were you closing anyway?' I asked George Ward, the landlord.

'I was closing anyway, Nick,' he said. 'It was a quiet night – I can do with an early night once in a while!'

We chatted about inconsequential things for a few minutes, but before I left, I asked, 'George, the lad who's just left with that girl: who is he?'

'Andrew Holdsworth,' he told me. 'And the girl is Sally Browning. He's from Craydale and she comes from Slemmington. Why, is he in bother?'

'Oh, no, it's just that I've seen him in various pubs over the months and he's never had a beer in front of him, even if all his

34

mates were knocking them back in fine style.'

'He doesn't drink alcohol, Nick, he never has, not a drop, but he's a lively, outgoing character. His pals have often tried to get him to change his mind, you know; they've used all the dodges but he's never given in. In fact, they formed a club and got him to join, all in an effort to try and get him to have a pint – and so far, they've failed.'

'The Castle Club?'

'Yes, that's the one. They meet at the King's Head in Ashfordly every market-day,' George told me. 'That's why it was formed. He's from a wealthy family, they're big farmers and agricultural implement dealers. Andrew's in line to inherit the lot one day, but ever since he could come into the pub, when he was eighteen, he's never let a drop of alcohol touch his lips. Most of those other lads he knocks around with are old schoolmates or lads he's met through work; they all enjoy a pint and a sing-song and although he'll sing with the best of them, they can't persuade him to enjoy a pint.'

'Is it against his religion?' I was curious to know. 'Or a medical thing?'

'Neither,' said George. 'He just refuses to

drink alcohol of any kind, not even a tiny sherry or champagne at a wedding. Nothing. He's as tee-total as anyone can be.'

'Well, I hope he sticks to his principles!' I laughed. 'It takes courage to set yourself apart from the crowd, but it seems he's capable of doing it – and his pals accept him in spite of it. I've seen him at the Castle Club at Ashfordly – he does enjoy himself with his orange squash...'

'That's Andrew,' smiled George. 'Determined as always.'

'Well, thanks for that snippet of information, George. Now you can lock up and go to bed!'

Over the following months, and indeed years, I came across Andrew Holdsworth on frequent occasions. Although his parents' farm and business premises were not on my patch, being only a mile or so across my western boundary, much of his social life and business dealings were done in and around Ashfordly. Apart from his attendances at Ashfordly market, he was a regular visitor to the Brewers Arms in Aidensfield, he bought petrol from Bernie Scripps's garage and had his car serviced there, and he, or his parents, could often be seen patronizing the post office and shop. In some ways, the Holdsworths were regarded as local people – indeed, they had lots of friends in Aidensfield, and I was not unduly surprised therefore, when one evening I received a telephone call from Jack Holdsworth, Andrew's father.

'Jack Holdsworth here, Mr Rhea.' The deep voice was pleasant and full of authority. 'I thought I'd give you a call about our Andrew's twenty-first birthday party.'

'Fine,' I said. 'So how can I help?'

'I've hired Aidensfield village hall,' he told me. 'There'll be a dance and a buffet supper for everybody, and I've asked George at the Brewers Arms if he'll set up a bar in the premises. He'll apply to the magistrates and see to all the legalities. I'll buy the first round for everyone, and then it's up to them. George says he'll need an occasional licence to sell the drinks in the village hall. It's on Saturday night, 6 September; I thought I'd better let you know what's going on.'

'Thanks for keeping me informed, I'll make a note in my diary,' I assured him.

'I thought that if you're on duty you could keep an eye on things. It's a private party, Mr Rhea, so I don't want gatecrashers or rowdies trying to muscle in, thinking it's a normal Saturday-night dance.'

'You'll have your own door stewards? If it's a private party?' I had no jurisdiction over private functions, although if problems spilt into the street, then of course, it was my problem.

'Oh, yes, I'll hire a couple of big chaps for the door. I don't anticipate trouble, they're all invited guests, but sometimes the presence of a uniform is a help if the clownish element tries to gain admittance.'

I checked my diary and found I was expected to be on duty that Saturday and assured Jack I would keep an eye on the place by patrolling the street outside the premises. The fact that there would be an occasional licence in force, to permit the sale of alcohol during the party, meant I had an obligation to supervise the place anyway. Jack thanked me and said if I popped into the hall during the festivities, say half past nine or so, there would be a plate of supper for me and even a glass of champagne if that was permitted for a constable on duty. Aidensfield Village Hall, with its beautifully sprung dance floor and ample facilities, was a very popular venue for hunt balls, wedding receptions and a host of private functions and so this kind of duty was a fairly common event for me, a mixture of police work and public relations on behalf of the constabulary.

On the night in question, I was performing a late shift – 9 p.m. until 1 a.m. – as part of my Saturday duties, having completed a four-hour stint between 9 a.m. and 1 p.m. that same morning. It was a lovely, mild September evening with just a hint of a warm breeze, ideal for a barbecue I felt, and so my evening's work promised to be very pleasant indeed. In full uniform, I walked down to the village from my hilltop police house. Already, the village hall car-park was full and cars were lining one side of the street. A few stragglers were heading for the hall, the men wearing evening suits and the ladies looking gorgeous in their long dresses. It was that kind of occasion.

A pair of large and impressive gentlemen were guarding the entrance to the hall and I made my presence known, saying I would be in the vicinity for a while and suggesting that, once the guests were inside, the doors be closed. An open village hall door is always an invitation to unwanted guests if music, drink and food are inside!

Jack Holdsworth spotted me as I chatted to his doormen and said, 'Don't forget, Mr

Rhea, nine-thirty! Everyone should be here by nine and supper will be served when I've said my piece. I hope you can join us.'

Having discovered that a dance was in progress, one or two drinkers from the near-by Brewers Arms did try to enter the hall but the doormen were up to their job and no one gained admission; then, a few minutes prior to 9.30 I walked in and suggested the doors now be closed. The doormen had had similar orders from Jack Holdsworth and so, once I was inside and heading for the laden tables, the double doors were closed and locked.

Any late-arriving guests might find themselves marooned, but that was their problem! The invitations had asked every-one to be present by nine at the latest.

Shortly after half past nine, with the crowd of some 300 people milling around, drink-ing, talking and laughing, Jack mounted the stage and rang a large brass hand bell at which everyone stood still and became silent. There was a handsome woman on one side – his wife Geraldine I was to discover – and on the other stood Andrew, looking smart, confident and mature in his dinner suit.

'Good evening all,' Jack said, his loud

voice not requiring a microphone. 'Glad you could all join us for Andrew's coming-of-age. This is the formal start of tonight's celebration, but at this point I have no intention of making a long speech. All I will say is that if you could collect a glass of champagne from the tables set up around the hall, we'll begin rightaway with a toast to Andrew. Then food will be available from the tables in the supper-room and there will be dancing afterwards. So, find yourselves a glass apiece!'

Without any supervisory officer to comment upon my actions, I decided I could sip a glass of champagne too and joined the queue; eventually, everyone had a glass and Jack rang his bell once more.

'I thought I would start the proceedings with a toast, while everyone can still hear me,' he smiled. 'On behalf of Geraldine and myself, I want to wish Andrew a very happy birthday indeed and to wish him every happiness for the future. We did have a family celebration at home this morning – he got his present then – but tonight is for his friends and other family members, cousins and so on.'

Jack said what a fine son Andrew had proven to be and after a few minutes, he asked us all to raise our glasses to toast the birthday boy. As the band struck up 'Happy Birthday to You', everyone sang the familiar words and raised their glasses to Andrew, me included. And then I realized Andrew had a glass of champagne in his hand and as we raised our glasses to him, he raised his glass towards us in a gesture of appreciation for our presence. After all his efforts to remain a teetotaller, he had succumbed on his twenty-first birthday!

But as the chatter recommenced to a burst of applause and the sinking of the champagne, the bell rang again. Jack's voice rose above the clamour.

'Those of us who know Andrew very well, and especially his pals from the Castle Club, will have noticed he has enjoyed a glass of champagne tonight. That is his first alcoholic drink since his eighteenth birthday – what few of you realize is that Andrew is not a teetotaller, but when he was eighteen, I made a bet with him. On his eighteenth birthday, the day he could legally buy drinks in the pub, I bet him five thousand pounds he could not resist alcohol until his twenty-first. Why did I do it? Well, when I was his age I drank a lot and gambled a lot and got myself into loads of trouble, giving my poor old dad a multitude of headaches and worries. I didn't want my own son to give me that kind of hassle and so I made that bet – well, Andrew has won. He's kept off the pop, but now he's a man, with all the responsibilities of a man – and so, Andrew, here's your reward – a cheque for five thousand pounds.'

Everyone applauded, including me and his pals from the Castle Club, and there were calls of 'Speech … speech…'

'I'd almost forgotten what champagne tasted like!' smiled Andrew, when everyone had quietened down. 'But it was lovely …I don't know what to say, except "Thanks, Dad" – it was a real challenge, especially under pressure from my Castle Club mates so what can I say now, except the next drinks are on me!'

I won't dwell on the rest of that evening, except to say that it all went exceedingly well without any kind of trouble. Andrew's proper birthday present was a blood-red Lotus Elite sports car and, although I left shortly after the meal, I later learnt that before the end of the evening, Andrew had announced his engagement to Juliet Ellis, his long-time girlfriend.

The next time I went into the Castle

Room of the King's Head in Ashfordly on market-day, the Castle Club members were in session as usual, except that this time Andrew Holdsworth had a pint of beer before him. Somehow, it didn't seem quite the same.

It was the blossoming of the Castle Club that highlighted a host of similar or even curious clubs and societies which were scattered around the North York Moors. These ranged from the wonderful Egton Bridge Old Gooseberry Society (whose members continue to grow and show giant gooseberries) to the Cleveland Bay Horse Society which sought to preserve that unique breed of horse, to minor clubs like the Elderberry Club for old folks and the Lyke Wake Walk Club whose members trekked across the highest and widest part of the North York Moors in twenty-four hours, using part of an ancient funeral processional route.

There were clubs specializing in budgerigars, rabbits, dahlias, fuchsias, watercolouring, wine-making and bottle collecting; there was, and still is, the Glaisdale and Lealholm Society for the Prosecution of Felons, several courts leet which remain active and the somewhat wonderful Chestnut Club. This was a club comprising ladies of a certain age (over seventy, in fact) and it had originated when someone had referred to them, when they met as a small private luncheon club, as old chestnuts. In retaliation, the ladies had said although a horse chestnut might be wrinkled and prickly on the shell, inside there is a rounded object which is wonderful to behold and exquisite to touch. Just like those ladies, in fact. And so they became the Chestnut Club, membership of which entailed finding an entire horse chestnut in its unbroken shell and bringing it to the meeting at which membership was sought. If membership of that applicant was approved, the chestnut was ceremonially broken open and the nut revealed in all its glory.

Due to the plethora of such clubs and societies in and around Aidensfield, I was therefore not very surprised to come across the Thumbstick Club. This consisted of twelve men, all more than sixty-five years of age, who met once a month for lunch at a small restaurant in a rather remote moorland hotel, the Laverock Hotel at Shelvingby. Each owned – and took to the lunch – a beautifully carved hazel thumbstick, the work of one of their founder members called Ken Ashby who lived in Ashfordly. The V-shaped fork of each stick was fashioned from the natural horns of moorland sheep and the tip of one prong was carved with the minute shape of a sign of the Zodiac.

The reason for there being twelve men was that only one example of each sign was permitted within club membership, and that sign had to correspond to the birthday sign of the stick's owner. Ken, the carver in chief, was born under the sign of Taurus and so his stick bore a bull on its V-prong. No other Taurean could therefore join the club until Ken died, and a like rule applied to all the other members. Only when a stick holder died was a replacement permitted, but first that new recruit had to persuade Ken Ashby to carve a stick especially for him. Ken would oblige – at a cost – and I understand that the new owners' initials were intricately carved somewhere in the delicate design on the fork of the V. Thus every stick was personalized and therefore unique. Apparently, no one had wondered what would happen in the future when Ken himself departed to his heavenly stick forest although it had been said, but never substantiated, that Ken had already carved a plentiful supply of sticks in advance, a selection of several all bearing various signs of the Zodiac, enough to last a century or more. Those new ones, of course, having been carved in advance, would not bear the initials of the new owner, but nonetheless they would ensure the continuity of the Thumbstick Club for many years.

Knowing of the club and its regular meetings, I never questioned its purpose but when my curiosity became too strong and I began to ponder the reason for this curious club, I discovered that it had only one purpose: to meet for lunch once a month. That prompted my next query – how did the club start?

My opportunity to find out came one Friday when I was undertaking one of my market-day duties in Ashfordly. I spotted Ken Ashby leaving the fish stall and he smiled in greeting. A small, neatly dressed man with a moustache and heavy spectacles, I knew him moderately well because he used to work in an ironmonger's shop in the town, retiring fairly recently.

'Hello, Mr Rhea,' he smiled. 'Not a bad day.'

We chatted about nothing in particular as

one tends to do on such occasions and then I said, 'Ken, can I ask you something?'

'Of course,' and his grey eyes twinkled.

'Your Thumbstick Club,' I began, deliberately referring to it as 'your' club. 'How did it start?'

'Are you hoping to join?' he chuckled. 'Because if you are, you're too young, we're all old codgers.'

'I couldn't join just yet, work commitments wouldn't let me even if you'd have me,' I smiled. 'No, it's not that, Ken. I was just curious how it all started; it seems such a wonderful idea.'

'It was all by accident, Mr Rhea,' he said. 'Years ago I carved myself a stick and my wife suggested I make it my very own by carving my birth sign on it. I'm Taurus, so I carved a bull on the horn which made one of the tips. Then a pal came along, retired he was, and asked if I could make him one, so I did. He was a bit surprised when I asked for his birth sign, but when I told him I'd include it on his stick, he was delighted. He was born under the sign of Cancer, so I added a crab.'

'And so a whole new industry was born?'

'Yes, quite suddenly other people began to ask for similar sticks, not all with birth signs carved on them, but usually with some personal object added – like their initials, the name of their house, something like an acorn or pear … I've added all sorts. Then one Saturday, a few of us, retired chaps like me, were in the pub having a pint and a chat and I realized that six of us had my carved sticks with them – and all six had a different sign of the Zodiac. Half jokingly, I suggested we form a club of old chaps wanting lunch together, and a chat about old times, with club membership being restricted to twelve men, each owning a stick carved by me and bearing a different sign of the Zodiac. Three of those other chaps immediately asked me to make them a stick, each with their own sign and suddenly, there were nine of us … it was easy to find the other three. So there we are, Mr Rhea: the history of the Thumbstick Club.'

'And that's all there is to it?'

'Nothing more complicated than that. We don't set out to raise money for charity; we don't discuss politics or religion or the issues of the day; we don't want to change society or write letters of complaint to the Press, or put pressure on politicians … we just pop out for lunch and amuse ourselves in whatever way we feel inclined at that moment, usually eating, drinking and telling old jokes.'

'It seems a good thing to join when I'm old enough!'

'There's a waiting list and we're very strict – we'll never have more than twelve members. It's a golden rule, we restrict ourselves to one for each sign of the Zodiac.'

'Thanks for telling me.' I turned to leave. 'It's satisfied my curiosity.'

'It will continue when I end my days,' he said. 'I've carved enough sticks in advance, without names or initials of course, but enough to last a few hundred years even if each member survives only ten years. And, I suppose, there's no reason why one member can't leave his stick to someone else in his will, provided they're of the same birth sign.'

'It's a very exclusive club!' I laughed.

'Extremely,' he said. 'That's why it is so good. See you, Mr Rhea.' And off he went.

I thought no more about the Thumbstick Club until one Saturday afternoon when I was patrolling in my Mini-van and received a radio call from Sergeant Craddock in Ashfordly.

'Ah, Constable Rhea.' His Welsh voice sounded crisp and clear over the air. 'Proceed immediately to the Laverock Hotel at Shelvingby, will you? Report of theft. Over.'

'Will co, Sergeant,' I acknowledged.

Fifteen minutes later, I pulled into the car-park to find a group of elderly men awaiting me, and among them I noticed Ken Ashby.

'Ah, Mr Rhea.' He was first to reach my van. 'Glad you could come so quickly.'

'So what's happened?' As I climbed out of my van, I looked at each of the men, wondering who had lost what. But Ken acted as spokesman.

'All our sticks have been stolen,' he sighed. 'All twelve.'

'Are you sure?' was my first reaction.

'Absolutely,' he confirmed. 'They've gone, every one of them. Vanished. I've asked around the hotel; we've searched all the likely places ourselves, but they've gone. Clean as a whistle.'

'Where from?'

'The stand in the entrance hall. It takes coats and umbrellas and such. We always put them there – we arrived about twelve and came for them after lunch, just before two, and they'd gone.'

'But who would steal a dozen thumb-sticks?' I frowned.

'A collector?' he suggested. 'Twelve hand-carved sticks, all identical except for that one little bit on the horn, and that little bit on each horn comprises a collection of all signs of the Zodiac.'

'But your sticks are unique,' I said. 'Not only for that reason, but also because each of your initials is also carved on the horn. You'd recognize your own stick, that's if we can trace them?'

'Oh, yes, there're no others anywhere like them.'

We went inside where the hotel owner, Simon Morden, was anxiously awaiting me and he explained how he'd searched the hotel and its outbuildings, thinking some-one might have hidden the sticks as a prank, but he'd found no sign of them. To satisfy my own wishes, I did likewise, searching all likely hiding places both indoors and out, but found nothing.

I took all their names and initials, made a note of the description of their sticks, then asked Mr Morden if anyone else had been in the hotel over the lunch period. No one had been in the bar area, he confirmed, but he suggested I talk to his receptionist – she'd gone home for lunch at one and was due back now. Even as we spoke, a Mini was coming up the drive; it halted outside and a young blonde woman emerged. As she entered, Simon Morden hailed her.

'Sue,' he said. 'Mr Rhea would like a word.'

Her name was Sue Henderson, she was thirty-two, married and lived in the village. I explained what had happened and she said no one else had been in for lunch and then she blanched and clapped a hand to her mouth.

'Oh dear, yes, there was a couple, a man and a woman. They came to reception, it would be about half past twelve, asking if we did bed and breakfast and so I said yes, a room was available and then I gave them our leaflet, showing charges and so on. As they were reading it, the phone rang, so I went to answer it, and when I'd finished, they'd gone. I saw the car leaving, going down the drive; I can see the drive from my office window. I thought no more about it.'

'And can you see the umbrella stand from reception?'

'No,' she said. 'The stand is inside the big entrance hall, reception is in the next hall, the inner hall. If I'm on the phone, I can't see the front door ... so, yes, they could have taken all the sticks, I suppose.'

'You can easily lift a dozen at once,' I said.

'I know, I've done it … so, Sue, can you describe them, or more important, their car?'

'Well, actually, I have the number, it's a habit I've got, taking car numbers. We often get your crime prevention people popping in, asking us to note car numbers, especially when there's a spate of people leaving without paying their bills. So I noted their number, force of habit I suppose.'

Simon Morden was delighted and so we trouped into Sue's office behind the reception desk where she found a scrap pad bearing a car number along with a description – it was a Ford Anglia, she'd noted, pale-blue in colour. I knew that if we were to recover the sticks or prosecute the thieves, we'd have to catch them in possession of the stolen property. If that couple were responsible, they'd had more than an hour's start – they could be thirty miles away or more, so that meant swift action with all mobiles and patrolling bobbies being alerted by radio, both in our force area and within adjoining counties and boroughs.

To cut short a long story, Hull City Police spotted the car as it was entering the town and it had all the sticks laid across its rear seat; they were recovered without damage and the pair were arrested. I was later to learn they were known to the police in Hull, often venturing into the countryside to steal whatever they could pick up – garden ornaments and tools, objects from souvenir shops, anything left outside houses like children's toys or even trikes, and one of their ploys was to visit hotels, ostensibly to ask about accommodation, and then to steal anything portable which happened to be available, such as objects on display like hunting horns or horse brasses, and even paintings and small sculptures. In this case, they'd not been seeking thumbsticks in particular – it just happened they were available at the time.

Ken and his Thumbstick Club members were delighted and rewarded Sue with a specially carved stick, ladies' size, with her birth sign carved on the horn, and then, quite unexpectedly, I was invited to join them at a lunch, as their special guest.

'It's our way of saying thank you,' Ken told me. 'I know you can't accept a reward for doing your duty, but the least we can do is invite you to lunch as our guest. Normally, we don't have guests, but we thought we could make an exception in this case.'

And so it was, one Saturday lunchtime when I was off duty, I went along to the

Laverock Hotel as the first guest of the Thumbstick Club. I enjoyed the occasion, but after the meal, Ken stood up and said, 'And now we would like to present Mr Rhea with a token of our appreciation. Nick, I do hope you can accept this thumbstick, it's been carved especially for you.'

And from beneath the table, he produced a beautiful hazel stick with the familiar horn V-shaped on top, but on the tip of each point he'd carved a miniature copy of a policeman's helmet.

'We know you are not allowed to accept gifts for doing your duty,' Ken said. 'So this is for your wife. Please accept it for her, with our compliments.'

'She'll be delighted to accept,' I said.

Chapter Three

Among the varied matters dealt with by police officers, animals frequently feature, dogs in particular. There are dozens of rules and regulations governing the ownership of dogs, and these range from the licensing system to the cruelty laws by way of regulations dealing with dangerous dogs. So far as I know, there are precious few corresponding rules about keeping, say, cats. Cats are a law unto themselves anyway and although the anti-cruelty legislation does consider them, there is no such crime as keeping a dangerous cat. After my stewardship of the Aidensfield beat, however, rules were made to regulate the keeping of dangerous animals, like lions, tigers and leopards. Big cats in other words – or very big dangerous cats to be precise.

So far as domestic cats were concerned, our involvement was often little more than rescuing them from roof tops or tall trees, or tripping over them while they slept in odd places as we patrolled on night duty, but there was one occasion when a cat got stuck beneath the floorboards of a partially built new house. The whole place was practically demolished in the attempts to rescue it, but it was never found. I think it had found its own way out, having surely been terrified by the banging and clattering which surrounded it. The house owner was left with a hefty bill – but it did help to know that the cat belonged to him anyway. Having lost that one, however, he took in a stray or two from a local cats' home, and we never knew whether or not his original pet had been permanently entombed in the house. Its possible fate reminded me of that ancient custom of burying a live creature in the foundations of new buildings to bring good fortune. I wondered if it might turn up as a ghost.

Our range of animal-linked duties included the cornering or even destruction of dangerous bulls or cows which escaped from their market-pens to rampage around towns and into the inevitable china shops (much to the delight of journalists and photographers) or we might have to hunt for a missing pet snake thought to have vanished down the toilet, an allegedly kidnapped hamster who mysteriously vanished from his hutch without the door being opened, a racehorse held for ransom, or even a pet rat which escaped and vanished in a departing furniture van. It was never seen again. I've coped with donkeys wandering through Ashfordly at night, pigs which got drunk on a diet of rotting apples, a pack of Canadian timber wolves which escaped from a zoo and waited in a bus shelter, and the clip-clop of a zebra's hooves behind me as I patrolled at night.

But I never expected to cope with a flock of dangerous geese at large in the middle of Aidensfield. My first intimation of this came in a telephone call from my former sergeant, Oscar Blaketon, who was now running Aidensfield Post Office.

'Nick.' He called me by my Christian name now that he was retired from the force. 'Nick, you'd better get yourself down to the village; there's a flock of geese in the middle of the road. They're having a go at pedestrians and causing a traffic jam. The old gander's a bit of a menace.'

'Whose are they?' was my first question.

'Search me, I don't know anyone who keeps so many geese. Just get yourself down here and do something about them. You might need help.'

59

'Shall I call in the Flying Squad?' I put to him.

'I'd say you need Gabriel's Hounds!' he retorted.

I smiled – I knew the legend of Gabriel's Hounds. When flocks of wild geese fly at night, they gabble continuously to one another and, in ancient times, people thought this peculiar, heavenly noise, somewhere beyond their vision, was the sound of the souls of unbaptized children crying as they wandered for ever through eternity. And because the noise was rather like a pack of foxhounds baying, the noise was also attributed to Gabriel's Hounds – although this might have been night-flying curlews.

Blaketon, of course, was suggesting I needed a pack of dogs to drive these geese back to wherever they had come from – but where had they come from? There was only one way to find out and so I popped my cap on my head and walked the half-mile or so into the village centre. When I arrived, the place seemed full of white geese, all babbling and squawking and flapping their wings as a small knot of people, including Blaketon, were trying to shoo them towards the village hall. But geese have no sense of community spirit like sheep – if you get one sheep to go through a gate or a hole in the wall, the rest will follow.

Geese don't behave like that and clearly they had no intention of being moved on – for one thing, the verges in the middle of the village were rich with lush grass, a wonderful source of food for a hungry goose. They were truly making a meal of it, nibbling as if there was no tomorrow, and all that the volunteer gooseherds succeeded in doing was making the geese go around in circles and get steadily more angry and upset. They'd found a wonderful place to sit and eat, and had no intention of leaving; they just wafted around in a haze of noise and flapping.

'I don't think you need me,' I shouted to Blaketon above the racket. 'You seem to be doing fine as it is! You're containing them very well.'

'We're not trying to do that, we want to herd them into the village hall car-park,' he told me. 'If we can get them in there, we can close the gates and detain them until we trace the owner.'

'It might be easier to leave them here,' I said. 'They seem happy enough on that grass. At least they can feed there and leave their droppings on the grass. They'll make an awful mess in the car-park.'

'But they're obstructing the highway, Nick, and one or two have had a go at passers-by, hissing and honking...'

'Well, my opinion, for what it's worth, is that it's best to leave them alone until we find the owner. If they're not harassed, they'll feed happily on this grass, and if they're only hissing and honking, they're not doing any harm to anyone. It's not as if they've committed grievous bodily harm upon a member of the public.'

'Owners of livestock are duty bound to make sure they are fenced in.' Blaketon began to sound more like his former self. 'It is an offence to allow livestock to stray on the public highway...'

'That only applies to cattle, horses, pigs, sheep and goats,' I reminded him. 'Not geese. They can fly, remember, like hens, bantams, ducks and even peacocks. You can't stop them straying. And that law about straying doesn't apply to a highway which passes over common land or through un-enclosed ground. So these geese are not committing an offence, and neither is their owner.'

'Well, I don't want noisy geese, who are not house-trained, wandering into my post office and messing all over the floor just because I leave the door standing open.' He sounded very determined. 'I still say it's your job to find the owner and get him to remove them. If they're not moved fairly soon, I'll take steps to have them impounded.'

'In that case you'll have to feed and water them!' I reminded him. 'If you impound animals, they become your responsibility.'

'But the owner will have to pay expenses,' he grinned. 'And he'll have to pay up before his geese are released. Or she, if it's a woman.'

'That's all right if you can find the owner,' I returned to the central problem. 'It's up to you to decide what to do, but how on earth you will persuade those geese to go into the village pound, I don't know. You can't even get them to enter the car-park and it's got a much wider gate. My advice is to leave them here while we hunt for their owner; there's enough grass to keep them happy for hours and it does need cutting. And look – now that everyone's backed off and the geese are left alone while we are deciding what to do, they've all calmed down. They probably think they live here now.'

They had calmed down and seemed

content to remain. They were nibbling quite happily at the grass along the verges and some had formed a small group on a patch of grass near the Aidensfield Stores. I didn't try to count them but estimated there would be about two dozen or perhaps thirty in total, and now that they had calmed down, the small band of Blaketon's gooseherds came across to us.

'I agree with the constable, I reckon we should leave them,' said one of them, an elderly gentleman who had patiently waited for the end of my debate with Blaketon. 'We were only making them worse by trying to round them up; they're fine now they've found this grass; they're off the road and not harming folks. So I'll be off.'

And so he turned away and, as he did so, the other half-dozen helpers, men and women, did likewise. The geese now settled down to feed and in fact two of them squatted on the ground, put their heads under their wings, and had a nap. Traffic was no longer interrupted by their presence and people were able to use the footpaths without the geese hissing at them. I decided to leave them there until I found their owner; in fact, I could see no sensible alternative.

'So how will you find the owner?' Blaketon asked. 'I thought I was the centre of all information in this place and I've no idea who they belong to. None of the farmers hereabouts keep such large numbers of geese. Most of them have just got one or two.'

'How did they get here?' I asked.

'No idea.' He spread his hands wide in a gesture of helplessness. 'There was I, having a quiet morning catching up with a bit of paperwork and suddenly the road outside is full of geese. They must have flown in from somewhere. It's not as if there's a pond here.'

'They're not wild ones,' I said. 'These are domestic geese; they're used to having people around. I'll make enquiries as I go on my patrols today.'

'So you want me to leave them here?'

'I do. There's enough food for them, Oscar; I think it's better than trying to drive them away. Even if we don't know who they belong to, we do know where they are. And if there's food, they'll stay.'

'All right,' he conceded. 'You've per-suaded me. You'll come back to keep me up to date?'

'I will,' I assured him.

I knew that several farmers in and around Aidensfield each kept a handful of geese, usually to act as highly efficient guards to their premises. Geese make wonderful guardians – they react to the slightest intrusion and noise, day or night, and with heads thrust forward and tongues hissing through their beaks, they will strut towards anyone perceived as a threat. They also make a tremendous noise and their antagonism is a great deterrent to wrongdoers. For all kinds of reasons, they are ideal sentries. One or two geese is usually enough, but an entire hissing flock heading towards you is daunting – it's enough to make any farmyard thief or burglar change his mind. I could understand passers-by not really wanting to upset the flock now grazing on Aidensfield's main street.

These were white geese which, to my limited knowledge, suggested they were the popular Embden breed which are sometimes interbred with English Whites to produce birds with healthy appetites and who put on weight very rapidly – ideal as Christmas feasts, or even for dinner at other times of the year. Embdens need lots of space with ample grass so they can feed and wander around with little restraint.

Furthermore, they like a stretch of water in which to swim. For all their size, however, they are most active and very capable fliers – so I knew that these birds could have come from anywhere within a radius of several miles. But there was no harm asking questions locally – I thought some nearby farmer or smallholder might know a colleague who kept a large number of Embdens. This enquiry would be my focus for today – as it happened, I had a quiet day ahead with no specific duty commitments and so I decided I could usefully employ myself on a not-so-wild goose chase.

Visiting a large number of farms, especially in outlying areas, is always a time-consuming affair due to their distance from the main centres of population, but also because most of the farmers and their wives are very hospitable. They love to have a chat and will offer visitors coffee, cakes and even liquor in return for half-an-hour's gossip. The outcome of that day's efforts, therefore, was that I spent an entire day nattering to farmers and their wives, eating their scones and drinking their coffee, without discovering who might own the flock of geese. Not many farmers kept flocks of geese at that time – turkeys had superseded them as a Christmas delicacy, and very few were as dependent upon geese as they had been in times past. Little more than a century earlier, geese had been central to the economy of a farm or even rural cottage. When I returned to Aidensfield, therefore, the geese were still enjoying themselves on the greenery which bordered the street, although several had squatted on the ground and appeared to be preparing to roost. I halted my van outside the post office and went in to acquaint Blaketon with the result of my enquiries.

He listened patiently and then said, 'Well, thanks for making the effort. I've been asking around too, but none of my customers knows where they've come from. So what now, Nick?'

'Leave them alone.' I could not think of any other sensible plan. 'It'll be dark soon and they'll go to sleep where they are, then we can have another think in the morning. I'm out and about in the Elsinby and Crampton area tomorrow, I'll pass the word around in those villages.'

'Have you seen Greengrass today?' was his next question. 'I thought he might know something about them but he's not been in.'

'I didn't get out to his ranch,' I had to

68

admit. 'But I could pop in tomorrow morning before I go to Elsinby.'

'Large scale goose dealing is something that might be in his line of business,' Blaketon considered. 'They might have escaped from his premises.'

'He's not been asking though, has he? Or searching the village for geese?'

'No, as I said, I've not set eyes on him today. If he does come in before I close, I'll ask him.'

'I'm off duty at five tonight,' I said. 'I might get into the pub for a drink, if he's there, I'll tackle him about it as well.'

And so I returned home leaving the geese to settle down for the night on the grass verges. At that point, they had been there for most of the day and it seems that, once settled, they had not caused any problems, other than the occasional hiss at an inquisitive schoolchild or dog.

In some ways, they were behaving like moorland sheep, eating and sleeping on the verges and keeping them trim. The residents of Aidensfield were completely accustomed to the sheep and I wondered how long it would take to be equally accustomed to the geese. After all, ponies lived wild in places like the New Forest and Exmoor, and not

69

far from Aidensfield was the village of Flaxton where cattle freely roamed the village greens, just as they did on the out-skirts of Beverley in the East Riding. It meant I was not too worried about the presence of those geese – in time, the villagers would surely find them acceptable.

As this day was one of those rare occasions when I finished work at five in the evening, I decided to visit the pub for a drink and asked Mary if she'd like to join me. She was able to find a baby-sitter at short notice and so we opted for a bar snack; by 8.30 we were sitting in a cosy corner of the Brewers' Arms with a log fire blazing in the grate and the babble of chatter around us. I was just settl-ing down to my chicken-and-chips in a basket when Claude Jeremiah Greengrass stomped in, hotly followed by his smelly lurcher, Alfred. He spotted me and padded in my direction looking anything but happy.

'I know you're not on duty,' were his first words, to which he added, 'I've been up to your house, but country coppers are sup-posed to be available twenty-four hours a day, if I'm not mistaken.'

'So what's your problem, Claude?'

'I've a crime to report...' he began.

'Right, well, in that case you'd better ring

Ashfordly Police Station.' I tried to stem his flow of words before it became too complicated. 'Sergeant Craddock will send someone out to see you.'

'Can't I just mention it to you?'

'Well, I'm off duty and I have none of the necessary documents with me, so all you have to do is pick up the phone and somebody will be with you in a few minutes. There's always somebody on patrol at this time of night...'

'Well, I thought I could just tell you and that would be it...'

'No, Claude, it's not as simple as that. There's a public phone in the hallway, use that and one of the Ashfordly constables will be with you in a minute or two, that's the proper way to go about it.'

'Well, the way I see it, the thief could be getting further and further away as we talk and I thought you fellows would drop everything and set up road blocks with your flashing blue lights and so on ... it's a rum do when you can't get the constabulary to do their job!'

I sighed as my chicken began to grow cold. 'So what's been stolen?' I asked.

'My geese,' he said. 'Two dozen of 'em, taken from that back paddock while I was away today.'

'Your geese?'

'Well, aye, of course they're my geese. I wouldn't be telling you this otherwise, would I? I only bought 'em yesterday and now they've gone. I can't earn a decent living if folks won't leave my things alone...'

'Have you come past the post office just now?'

'No, I came in from Eltering, I've been away on business all day and got back to find I've been robbed.'

'Claude,' I said, 'if you would care to walk along the village towards the post office, you'll find a flock of geese sitting on the grass verge. They've been there all day, hissing at passers-by and honking at cars and getting in the way of traffic.'

'My geese?'

'Well, I can't think who else they might belong to. Nobody knows who they belong to or where they've come from, and when I came along recently, they were all settling down for the night, having cropped our verges very neatly, I might add.'

'Aye, well, the parish council might care to pay me for grass cutting services, mebbe?'

'Or they might send you a bill for cleaning up the mess on the road and footpaths.'

'So how did they get out, Constable? I closed the gate when I put 'em in, yesterday that was, you'd think they'd not want to wander off, there's plenty of fresh grass up there and a bit of a beck they can swim in.'

'Geese have wings, Claude, they can fly.'

'I'll have to clip their wings then, if they're going to keep doing this. Anyroad, thanks. I'll go and find them. Come on, Alfred.'

'What are you going to do?' I asked him.

'I'm going to take 'em home,' he said. 'Alfred's as good as any sheepdog when it comes to rounding up geese. We'll get 'em gathered up and he can drive 'em along to my spot, no trouble.'

'Do you want any help?' I asked. 'It is dark, remember.'

'No, you enjoy your chicken-and-chips, me and Alfred can cope. It's dark so they'll be no trouble. Me and Alfred will just round 'em up and they'll all be safe and sound in that paddock in less than half an hour. Then I might pop in for a pint .... I'm glad they weren't pinched, mind.'

'Me too,' I said with some relief.

Claude, with Alfred at his heels, swept out of the pub and I settled down to finish my meal. I reckoned it would take him five minutes to reach the roosting geese, and then I'd expect to hear him herding them past the pub within a further ten minutes or so. I wasn't sure how the geese would respond to being roused and herded along the street at night, but I was sure they would make a lot of noise. As I finished my meal, some time later than Mary had completed hers, Blaketon walked in. I was already heading for the bar and offered to buy him a pint. He accepted.

'I've just seen Greengrass,' he smiled. 'Heading for those geese; they're his, he tells me. All I can say is I'm pleased he's going to shift them now; I didn't relish having them wake me up at the crack of dawn with their honking and hissing.'

'He seems to think he and Alfred can cope with them,' I smiled. 'He thought they'd been stolen. I nearly had a crime on my hands!'

'No more wild goose chases for you, then?' He picked up his pint and said, 'Cheers.'

I responded and returned to Mary; we left our table and joined Blaketon at the bar for a convivial evening, happy that the great goose affair of Aidensfield had been satisfactorily resolved. But, minutes later, Greengrass barged in looking furious. 'I'll have a pint, George, and quick. I need one!'

'Have it on me, Claude,' I said. 'To celebrate the return of your stolen property.'

'Return!' he snarled. 'They've not returned. Me and Alfred got down there – we found 'em like you said – and when that big gander saw Alfred he had a go at him; Alfred snapped back and nipped that daft goose on his tail and so he took off … and all those daft birds took off after him.'

'So where have they gone?' asked Blaketon.

'How should I know? It's dark out there. All I know is they took off in the dark and flew somewhere out Ashfordly way … honking and hissing they were … like Gabriel's Hounds.'

'So if I get a report of Gabriel's Hounds flying over Aidensfield tonight, I'll know it's a true account!' I laughed.

'It's not funny!' he snapped, sipping at the pint I had bought him. 'I paid good money for those geese. How can I find 'em now?'

'You could always ring the police,' I grinned. 'And report them as lost property. I'm sure Sergeant Craddock would love to go out and hunt them.'

'There'll be no Christmas dinners in this village if I don't find 'em,' Claude muttered.

'So how far can a goose fly at night?'

'Oh, not very far,' I told him. 'Most of our wild geese come in from the Arctic Circle, Spitzbergen and Greenland and places like that, but some take a rest in Scotland before heading this way. But I think you'd better report them as lost property, just in case they decide to land in Ashfordly market-place.'

Claude's geese were found on a farm pond near Ploatby and so far as I know, he allowed them to remain there. As he told me, 'Every time they see Alfred, they jump into the water and Alfred's not a very good swimmer. He's not much good at rounding up ducks on water so I reckon he'd be useless with geese. I don't think it's a good idea to try and round 'em up on land, they could fly off anywhere, Iceland, Canada, Norway, and I don't want to go chasing 'em in those foreign parts, so I've told that farmer he can have my entire flock at a good price. Mind, he's not paid me yet, but at least I know where they are.'

'No more wild goose chases, then?' I grinned.

Alfred's natural propensity for chasing things resurrected itself at Ashfordly market

76

one wet and foggy Friday in September. The atrocious weather made things appear more like a November day and this had had a detrimental effect upon the market because so few people had attended. Nonetheless, a band of sturdy stallholders had turned up, suitably protected against the heavy drizzle, to gallantly await their regular customers.

I happened to be on duty in Ashfordly that day and, as I patrolled the near deserted market-place noted, among the stallholders, the familiar figure of Claude Jeremiah Greengrass. He had prepared a large wooden table over which he had erected a brightly coloured red and white awning, and upon his stall was a selection of Greengrass produce – some beetroot, cabbages, carrots, potatoes and broad beans, as well as some fruit – apples, plums and pears. It was all spread out beneath handwritten notices which said, 'High-class home-grown produce' followed by Claude's name, address and telephone number. Claude wore his familiar old army greatcoat, but lying beneath his stall, on an old hearth rug, was Alfred, Claude's faithful, but smelly, lurcher dog. Both master and dog looked bored in the extreme.

'Good morning, Claude.' I tried to sound

cheery and happy to see him.

'What's good about it?' he muttered. 'I'd have been better off at home putting this lot outside my gate. Mebbe I'd have had a few sales from passing motorists or lorry drivers.'

'It might fair up.' I gazed skywards in the vain hope that things might improve. 'Besides, it's early yet, folks won't have taken to the roads yet.'

'If they have, they'll have gone the other way,' he grumbled. 'The forecast said it would be fine over the Pennines but cold and wet over our moors. There's nowt like a drop of rain for stopping tourists from touring and market-attenders from attending markets.'

I plodded on, taking in the various stalls and their less-than-cheery owners and decided it might be an idea if I slipped into one of the hotels. Inside, it would be warm and dry, and I could explain that I'd just popped in to check that no confidence trickers had been guests and to warn them about such travelling villains. If my luck was in, a cup of coffee and a biscuit might appear as a bonus! And so it did. As I entered the stately reception area of the Swan, Jill Breckon, the receptionist, smiled and said, 'Sit down, Mr Rhea, I'll get you a coffee and a chocolate biscuit. Milk but no sugar, isn't it?'

And so I sheltered from the cold and wet as I told Jill about a pair of confidence tricksters who were known to be in the north-east of England, their MO being to project themselves as a wealthy married couple. They spent time at good-class hotels – three or four nights as a rule – and then left without paying. We didn't have much information about them, although we had a vague description. I provided her with as much detail as I could and remained for about three-quarters of an hour, chatting to Jill and enjoying my unscheduled break. But I could not shirk my market-day duties and so, thanking her for her hospitality, I returned to the cold exterior. As I crossed the road, I was just in time to see Alfred hurtle from his bed beneath Claude's table and charge at a nearby stall, yapping and snarling as he went.

Pandemonium followed. I was too far away to gain a clear impression of what happened, and my view was obstructed by market-stalls and people, but as I hurried forward, I saw Alfred barking and galloping along one of the aisles amidst shouts and curses from stallholders. In his desperate rush, he was knocking over displays of flowers and plant pots, upskittling boxes of eggs and fruit and getting tangled in some displays of nightgowns and knickers. Then he leapt on to a stall.

By this stage, I was back within the market-place and could see what was on that stall – it held several pet rabbits in hutches and some of the hutches had little wire-netting runs attached to them. In those runs were some baby rabbits and some adults, and it was an adult which had caught Alfred's attention. It was a big white rabbit and I could see it hopping about in its modest enclosure on the stall, a very prominent sight, especially for a dog which was not secured or held on a lead. Before anyone could stop him, Alfred took a flying leap onto the stall, snarling and growling, and his actions sent the wire-netting run spinning to the ground whereupon the rabbit broke loose. The run, of course, had no base. Now there was nothing to detain the rabbit and with a ferocious dog making threatening noises, the rabbit did what rabbits normally do – it fled.

Wild rabbits are particularly adept at weaving and dodging, and equally proficient at finding secure hiding places and it seems that this domestic rabbit had lost none of those natural survival skills. Survival was its only thought at that moment and so it raced underneath a stall full of shoes and slippers, shot out the other side and under a stall beneath which were arrangements of mugs, cups, saucers and plates, and then towards the main fruit and vegetable stall. Boxes of oranges, plums and apples, as well as other things like pomegranates, grapes, potatoes and carrots were arranged both on the stall and around its base and it was through a gap between the oranges and plums that the rabbit bolted in its search for safe haven. I think it felt it would be safe under the stall among all those boxes and sacks. But Alfred had other ideas.

At this point, I was now among a crowd of traders and customers who were trying, without success, to catch Alfred and also to drive the rabbit into some secure place, but all their efforts were in vain. With Green-grass shouting and cursing while doing his best to call off his rampaging hound, Alfred scattered shoes and slippers, knocked over crates of crockery with resounding crashes, upskittled boxes of apples and oranges and shocked some maiden ladies by darting between their legs in his mad urge to catch the white rabbit.

Just as someone was about to grab Alfred by the scruff of his neck as he sniffed and pawed at some boxes of vegetables, he gave them the slip, knocked aside the boxes and found himself beneath the fruit stall. He knew the rabbit was under there somewhere – he could smell it – but when the hiding rabbit realized Alfred was rather too close for comfort, it darted from its hiding place among some empty boxes and sped under the lorry which formed the rear of the stall, then immediately bolted out at the other side. Several people shouted; they tried to catch the terrified rabbit to save it from a fate worse than death, but Alfred realized what was afoot, abandoned his search beneath the stall and hurtled out to see the rabbit speeding across the market-place with a handful of people, including Claude Jeremiah Greengrass, in hue and cry after it.

I was in time to see the rabbit galloping across the road which bordered one side of the market-square. Alfred was only yards behind and, as he hurtled across the road, a bus and a lorry braked to a halt with their drivers shouting obscenities at the dog but Alfred ignored them and sped ever onwards.

By chance, the door of the King's Head was standing open as a delivery of soft drinks and spirits was being carried inside and the sight of the dark and welcoming hole was enough for the panic-stricken rabbit. It bolted indoors and vanished into the dark interior just as Alfred gained the footpath outside. Within seconds, he was inside too, barking and snarling and sniffing as he tried to determine the route taken by his quarry. But there were people about, customers and delivery men and, as the rabbit vanished, Alfred was left standing in the entrance passage, wondering which way he should now go. To the right were two bars; to the left was another bar leading into yet further rooms; ahead was reception and, if you turned right, there were the toilets and a passage leading to the foot of the staircase, and beyond that, another wide corridor heading for the kitchen, the ballroom and the dining-room open to residents and non-residents alike. Beyond that was the garden and the hotel car-park.

Being an old building full of corridors, passages and doorways, it was very like a rabbit warren – ideal for the rabbit I felt – and, as I arrived at the door, the landlord, John Ramsey, was emerging, looking utterly baffled. In his mid-forties, he was fairly new to this role but had already built up a good reputation for the hotel, both from the food and the accommodation aspects.

'That dog of Greengrass's has just hurtled past me. I couldn't stop it, it's gone into the dining-room.' He looked in surprise at the gathering of people outside. 'What's going on?'

'Have you seen a white rabbit?' I asked in all seriousness.

'Is this something out of *Alice in Wonderland?*' he grinned.

'No, it's not, but you've got a white rabbit somewhere in here, and that dog is looking for it. It's already demolished half the market-stalls and terrified some old ladies, and if that rabbit gets among your bottles...'

Claude, panting heavily, now arrived. 'Where is he? I'll skin that dog alive when I get my hands on him.'

'Claude,' I said, 'Alfred has gone through to the dining-room area. You'd better find him and get hold of him before he finds the rabbit.'

'Why, where's the rabbit?'

'We don't know. I think the first thing is to get that dog of yours out before it does any more damage.'

'Right, sorry about this, John, but dogs will be dogs and Alfred does enjoy a good rabbit chase... Alfred, Alfred, where are you? Come here ... here boy, here...' and, Claude headed into the depths of the hotel, calling for his dog to come to heel. I explained to John Ramsey what had already occurred and he agreed that the best thing for us now, was to get Alfred out of the hotel and into some secure place like Claude's lorry, and then to make a methodical search for the terrified, and concealed, white rabbit. I also suggested to Claude that he have words with his fellow stallholders to see about paying for the damage, but Claude did not seem too keen to follow that route. I got the impression he thought it prudent merely to vanish in search of his dog, and to clear away his stall later in the day when everyone else had gone home. He also expressed a feeling that he might not come to the market next week.

Locating Alfred was not too difficult – he was in the dining-room, snuffling under the tables all of which bore long cloths – and we left that to Claude, feeling that too many of us might terrify the dog into bolting upstairs or through the kitchen area and so, after a very short time, Claude found Alfred, slipped a lead onto his collar and removed him from the hotel with due apologies. Luckily, no harm or damage had resulted from his visit to the hotel, even if the market-place remained in a state of turmoil.

The white rabbit, however, was still somewhere inside the hotel. With eighteen bedrooms, umpteen bathrooms and a conference room upstairs, plus all the ground-floor accommodation and cellars, it would not be an easy matter finding it. A rabbit in full gallop can pass through the legs of any crowd of people and, as many of the internal doors stood open, the rabbit might be anywhere. Although it was not really my problem, I offered to help John make a thorough search; being market-day, he was busy with customers, and so I had a hurried meeting with him, in the dining-room, as we decided the best strategy for the hunt.

As all doors of the upstairs rooms would be closed, we decided to concentrate on the ground floor, and with Alfred being found in the dining-room, we began in that area. But even as John and I entered the dining-room, a small boy, aged about five, appeared from the garden. He was carrying a white rabbit.

'Look what I found, Dad, he was in the garden, eating your lettuces.'

The rabbit was now quiet and calm, and appeared to be totally content to sit in the arms of the little boy.

'Where was he, Mark?'

'Outside, Dad, eating lettuces. Isn't he lovely? Can I keep him?'

'He doesn't belong to us, Mark, he belongs to a man on the market...'

'Look,' I said, 'I don't think it would be a good idea to carry that rabbit back to the market, not until Claude's dog has gone and things have returned to normal. Have you somewhere you can keep him safe for a few minutes? I'll go and inform the owner where he is and he can collect him when he's ready.'

'There is a hutch in the garden; it was there when we took over. Mark, we'll put the rabbit in the hutch...'

'Can we keep him, Dad? Can we? He likes me, you can see he likes me.'

'It was for sale in the market,' I told John. 'That's between you and the rabbit's owner. Well, I'll be off now.'

I found the stallholder and told him where he could find his rabbit, explaining about the little boy and how the rabbit was now calm and content to be with the child.

'He's used to children, Mr Rhea; the family who owned him have left the area and asked me to sell him as they've nowhere to keep him now. Let me talk to that boy at the Kings Head. I'm sure we can come to some arrangement – if his father will allow it.'

And so the great market-day rabbit hunt ended satisfactorily. John bought the rabbit for his son and the next time I paid a visit to the King's Head, I was shown the rabbit – named Clarence – in his newly painted hutch.

He seemed very happy in his new home in the hotel garden but I don't think Claude ever paid for the chaos caused by Alfred in his high-spirited market-day gallop.

Chapter Four

Early morning in Aidensfield, especially during the summer months, was a wonderful time and its charms were such that many people were persuaded to rush out of doors at sunrise to enjoy the rousing freshness of the new day. During those first few minutes after dawn, even at the height of summer, there was an exhilarating tingle in the air, a sharp freshness which could be guaranteed to bring a touch of colour to anyone's cheeks. Even though it was often a struggle to climb out of bed, the truth was I enjoyed those occasions when I had to undertake an early morning tour of duty. There were times I had to persuade myself that I was being paid to enjoy this kind of work.

In spite of that, to be out of doors before six in the morning was not something I did every day – my irregular working hours denied me that privilege – but whenever I found myself walking along the street before the milkman had delivered his wares, or the baker had begun to produce his cakes and bread, the experience was invariably memorable. As an added bonus, while the sun was climbing over those heathery heights to spread light where darkness had been swept away, I might be fortunate enough to spot some browsing deer or a fox or a badger, but I was more likely to encounter some of those sturdy folk who regularly rose from their beds before dawn every day to either run, walk and cycle, or to exercise their horses before starting their workaday exertions. Such activity at dawn never failed to amaze me. Hard-working people would find the energy to rise from their beds at some unearthly hour like 5 a.m. and then spend the next couple of hours in very energetic pursuits.

Some would run across the moors, others would resort to cycling to Ashfordly and back before breakfast just to fill their lungs with fresh air and to get all their working bits fully operational ahead of a busy day. The harder they worked, or the more pressurized and demanding their day job, the more they seemed to gallop around the moors in shorts or track suits at dawn. Some would set themselves targets – one did a round trip on his pedal cycle, executing a circular tour from Aidensfield to Briggsby, and then across the moors towards Harrowby before descending to Maddleskirk and back to Aidensfield. Each day he tried to beat his previous best time for the trip. Another did a daily walk from Aidensfield to Elsinby and back – about four miles in total – again trying each time to produce a faster time for his outing. In both these cases, those fellows went on to fulfil a busy day in their respective places of work.

Not all were youngsters either. One elderly lady, in her seventies I guessed, always rose at 5.30 a.m. to take her three dogs for a gallop across the moors, saying it was wonderful for the dogs and just as wonderful for herself, although I doubt if she actually galloped. I must admit she always looked healthy and happy, and so did her three spaniels. And there was an old man, well into his eighties, who told me, 'I used to run around the cricket field every morning before breakfast, but now I can only get halfway round and then I have to turn back.' Another man in his seventies told me he did a hundred press-ups every morning, while yet another of similar age had a room full of weight-lifting equipment which he used every day of his life.

It dawned upon me that these people,

whatever their age, were all trying to maintain their health, but there was something else. They were attempting small but important personal achievements or improvements to their lives and even if their day job (or their retirement) was mundane, boring or unrewarding, they could rest in the knowledge they had attained something worthwhile, like knocking a minute off their daily walk time, reducing the time of their cycle trip by a couple of minutes, or completing a routine impossible to others of similar age. I realized that these examples of personal achievement, however irrelevant to the rest of us, were important to them even if they did not achieve happiness, success or promotion at work. This range of domestic triumphs might even be some form of compensation for an otherwise dull or uninspiring life or work.

But what might be a personal achievement for some was occasionally far from being worthwhile in the eyes of others. One example of this was Twelve-pint Pete. Peter Stanley Yardley, to give him his full name, was a building-site labourer in his late thirties, a tall, gangly man with a head of untidily long, dark hair which flourished around his neck but produced very little on top. Thus he had a strikingly tanned bald head, the result of his outdoor work. It looked like one end of an ostrich egg poking through a nest of black feathers. He also sported a thick Mexican-style moustache and occasionally cultivated a small goatee beard.

From my point of view as a policeman, Pete never caused me any trouble. He did not own a car but travelled everywhere on his pedal cycle, except when he was going to work, in which case he used his employer's lorry, or bus.

This official transport carried him to building sites all over the north-east of England – he went wherever he could find work. Unmarried, he lived with his mother in a council house at Elsinby. She was a widow, her late husband having been a lorry driver employed by the county council, and Pete helped her in the house and garden. He also contributed to the household expenses – but apart from that, he had no cares or worries. His mother saw to all his domestic needs, like washing his clothes, changing his bed and cooking his meals. Pete was a capable and hard worker, so I was told, one who could be relied upon to be honest in his dealings with others, and very conscientious in his work-a-day routine. Those for whom he worked were full of praise for him, and he never had difficulty finding employment. Pete had no girlfriend, no romance and no hobbies or outside interests – except for drinking pints of beer. That was his only hobby and it was something he undertook every night of the week, being quite prepared to work overtime or at weekends to fuel his sole interest.

I would see Pete usually in the Hopbind Inn at Elsinby but sometimes in other pubs within cycling distance of his home, and there is little doubt he was popular with his drinking pals. They would sit around the table and chat, sometimes breaking off to play darts or dominoes, but Pete was usually the centre of attention because of his nightly ritual. He would drink twelve pints of beer every evening. That was one and a half gallons by my reckoning, just short of seven litres in metric measure – in other words, a lot of beer. I had no idea where he put it all; I could not comprehend anyone being able to accommodate so much extra liquid in their body.

It amazed me that he could drink all that in the course of a single evening, but I never saw him drunk or incapable. He was able to tolerate that huge quantity without any apparent decline in his senses or stability. And he never seemed to put on weight. He remained rather slim without any sign of a beer belly.

Quite often, I would see him leaving the Hopbind at closing time to walk the short distance home. He was never rowdy or unsteady on his feet, although I did feel sometimes that his speech was slightly slurred, but whenever he spotted me, he would say, 'I've had twelve pints again tonight, Mr Rhea.' He said this in the same way that a man might say, 'I scored a century last Saturday in our league cricket match', or 'I swam a hundred lengths last night', or 'I cycled from Ashfordly to Aidensfield in twelve minutes'. For Pete, this was his personal achievement, his claim to fame, because his pals always counted his pints and so he had developed some kind of reputation, and having created that kind of aura, he was then compelled to maintain it. Not surprisingly, therefore, he became known as Twelve-pint Pete and he seemed keen to live up to the reputation he had secured. If Pete was drinking as newcomers entered the pub, maybe tourists and holidaymakers, he would be exhibited by his pals as some kind of local celebrity where-upon gullible visitors would play their part by buying him a pint or two. And Pete would respond by proving he could drink twelve pints during the evening. His display was rather like feeding monkeys and watching them devour one's offerings. It is said though that everyone enjoys fifteen minutes of fame – and this was Pete's, although it has to be said it took longer than fifteen minutes to complete his showpiece.

Although the drink-driving laws had, by that time, come into force, I was not concerned about Pete's culpability because he didn't drive a car or motor vehicle of any kind. Sometimes he rode a pedal cycle and although there was a summary offence of riding a pedal cycle while unfit through alcohol – and 'unfit' meant not having proper control of the machine – I never saw Pete in such a state. Because he wasn't troublesome or incapable, I saw no legal reason to try and curb his drinking. Although his health was no official concern of mine, several well-meaning people, including the local GP, Dr Archie McGee, suggested he reduced his capacity on health grounds. I had words with him too, suggest-ing he had proved his skills and that there was no need to continue. But Pete thought he was invincible – and besides, what else could he do to impress people? He could not sing, or play the piano, or score well at darts … just as other people had a variety of skills and talents by which they could impress or entertain others, so Pete continued with his – the drinking of twelve pints of best bitter per evening.

One or two local people, who had some kind of affection for Pete, or perhaps a degree of concern, tried to wean him off his beer-drinking by suggesting he might take up a different hobby. One of them, for reasons best known to himself, thought archery might suit Pete's talents, but Pete reckoned he knew nothing about clouts or fletching. Another thought Pete might like to begin a collection of some kind – horse brasses, beer-pump handles, lemonade bottles with glass marbles in their necks, triangular-shaped beer mats, or dwyles bearing Yorkshire landscapes, but none of these appealed to Twelve-pint Pete. He was quite content to live up to and further his name by demonstrating how he coped with his renowned thirst.

Then Pete met his match. By chance, it happened on a Wednesday evening when I was off duty and enjoying a bar snack and a drink with a colleague in the Hopbind Inn at Elsinby. My friend, Alan, and his wife, Pat, were staying in the area, and Pat had gone to visit her sister who had just produced twins in Ashfordly Maternity Hospital. As persons of the male gender were not made very welcome in such hospitals at that time, Alan had opted to join me for a drink and chat to reminisce about former times. He was a policeman in Hull and we had become friends during our Initial Course at the Police Training Centre. That Wednesday, therefore, we were sitting in a corner of the bar and I spotted Pete and his cronies at the counter, laughing and chatting as usual. Pete was in fine form and when we arrived, was about to begin his fourth pint. By the time we had finished our meal, he was on to Pint No. 9 and then, shortly before closing-time, a group of four, stocky, middle-aged men arrived. They headed for the bar and established them-selves next to Pete's crowd, and soon, as was their practice, Pete's pals began to chat with the newcomers, whereupon Pete's capacity for sinking pints – albeit not at speed – became the topic of conversation. By this stage, Pete was sinking Pint No. 10 with a view to consuming the remaining two before the landlord called 'Time.'

As Alan and I were relaxing after our meal, there was a lull in the conversation, and I heard one of the newcomers say, 'So how good are you with a Yard of Ale?'

'Never tried it,' said Pete, with his customary honesty.

'Stan here is the champion of York,' continued the spokesman, tapping his pal on the shoulder. 'He can sink a Yard of Ale in eight seconds.'

'I don't like to rush my drinks,' Pete said with a certain wisdom. 'I prefer to savour my bitter, not to drink it without it touching the sides.'

'Aye but this is real skill,' the man continued. 'You have to empty the Yard of Ale without spilling a drop ... that takes real skill. Not many can do that, most who try finish up with beer all over their faces and shoulders.'

'You could do it, Pete,' cried one of his supporters. 'If anybody can drain a Yard of Ale without spilling a drop, you can! Take your time, Pete; you don't have to try and beat any records. Just empty it without spilling, that's the main thing to do.'

'Go on, Pete, show him you can do it!'

And in moments, Pete's pals had persuaded George, the landlord, to take the Yard of Ale down from its resting place on a beam above the bar, wash it and then fill it with beer. For those not accustomed to this object, it is made of glass and looks like a basic trumpet with a splayed-out opening at one end, just like the mouth of a trumpet, while the other end consists of a glass ball or bulb. The whole thing is a yard long, hence its name (.9144 of a metre), but the bulbous end may vary in size between models. The most common example holds two and a half pints of beer (1.42 litres), but the size of the bulb may vary somewhat – some Yards of Ale can hold three pints (1.70 litres).

Many pubs have at least one example of this instrument in the bar, more often displayed as a decorative object. Usually, it hangs on a beam where it gathers dust as the years go by, although in some areas these Yards are used in sporting challenges to determine who can drink the contents in the shortest time. During my period at Aidensfield, a Mr Lawrence Hill of Bolton in Lancashire drank a Yard of Ale (2.5 pint size) in 6.5 seconds. He achieved this on 17 December 1964 – and it had to be done in one continuous draught without spilling a drop. The tricky time is when there is about half a pint left in the bulb and the end of the Yard has to be elevated, with the bulb in the air, so that those final contents can be drained. That is when it gushes out and rushes down the tube to half drown the drinker. To correctly drink a Yard of Ale demands substantial skills gained by lots of practice.

Faced with a challenge of the like he had never before encountered, Pete was uncertain, but had the wit to say to the opposition, 'Show me how it's done.'

The newcomer called Stan stepped forward, asked George to fill the Yard to the brim, paid his money and then began his demonstration. As his lips connected with the mouth of the trumpet-shaped glass, his mates began to cheer; he drew the beer into his mouth like a suction pump, gradually elevating the tube until it was flowing into him like a rivulet vanishing down a drain, and then came the tricky bit – with a small quantity left in the bulb, he lifted it higher than his head and suddenly, it was empty. It had taken but a few seconds. He'd coped without the residue swishing down the tube into his face and hadn't spilled a drop.

'Easy, eh? Stan could be world champion

if he wanted,' said one of his mates. 'He just needs a bit more practice and mebbe a spot of coaching and intensified training.'

'Come on, Pete,' shouted someone in the bar. 'You can do that!'

'No,' he shook his head. 'No, that's not for me.'

'Come on, Pete, you can't let strangers get the better of you; there's no finer ale-supper in these parts ... you can't let us down, can he, lads?'

'No!' came the response.

The outcome of this banter was that Twelve-pint Pete was propelled into an arena in which he had no desire to perform. The Yard of Ale was filled at the pump and pushed into his unwilling hands and, to the cheers of the assembled multitude, Pete raised the glass and tried to emulate Stan. He failed. As he lifted the trumpet-shaped container, the beer washed down the tube, overflowed around his mouth and washed all over his face. Everyone cheered his efforts and laughed at his failure. George, the landlord, told him not to worry about the beer spilt on to the stone floor and although everyone pressed him to try again, Pete shook his head.

'I've had my share for tonight,' he told

them. 'Twelve pints – counting the bit I drank from the Yard. No more. I make a rule, no more than twelve.'

'We'll be back,' said Stan, the man from York. 'In a month from now. Mebbe you'll give us another go? Loser pays all or something?'

'I'll think about it,' Pete said quietly. 'As I said, I'm not one for supping it fast, I like to savour it...'

'There's no time to savour a Yard of Ale,' said Stan. 'It has to be downed as fast as you can. But we'll be back. See you again.'

And with that, the newcomers left.

I could see that Pete was rather embarrassed by what he regarded as a beer-drinking failure on his part and I wondered if he felt that his reputation was now tarnished. After all, until that moment, he had been beer-drinker supreme, at least in Elsinby and the neighbourhood. Now he had been shown another skill and he had failed.

Alan went off to collect his wife and I made my way back to my police house on the hill. Three or four days later, I called at the Hopbind on a routine duty visit and George made reference to that evening.

'It's years since that Yard of Ale was used,'

he told me. 'There was a time when it was all the rage, everyone was having a go and then they got fed up and the challenges came to a halt. It's been hanging in my bar for ages without ever being filled up and used, but you know what's happened?'

'Go on, surprise me!'

'Pete asked me to find him one. I've a pal in Beverley who collects oddments from pubs and bars, memorabilia like disused beer pumps, rare beer bottles, horse brasses, advertising pieces like the Guinness toucan, the Johnny Walker striding man and so on, and he had a spare Yard. I got one when I saw him yesterday and Pete picked it up last night. He's taken it home.'

'As a souvenir?' I smiled.

'No, to practise with. He's bought some bottles of beer to fill it so he can practise at home. He says he wants to come back when he'd had a bit of practice and show that Stan, the man from York, how to sink a Yard of Ale.'

And so it was that Twelve-pint Pete began to spend time at home, practising his skills at draining the yard of Ale by using bottled beer in the privacy of his own surrounds. I never saw him during those days and weeks of training although I heard, through gossip from the regulars in the Hopbind, that on occasions he would take his own Yard into the bar to demonstrate his new skill. With great encouragement from his peers, he perfected the art of swigging a Yard of Ale without spilling a drop while downing it in one long, smooth operation. He would provide a demonstration towards the end of most evenings, but would always ensure he never drank more than his twelve pints. In fact, due to his new talent, he often drank less than twelve pints. He would consume the 2.5 pints after drinking nine pint glasses of bitter thus making his evening's intake 11.5 pints, a slight reduction on his normal intake.

Then the inevitable happened. Stan, the man from York, and his friends returned one Wednesday evening. Pete and his companions were already installed with Pete about to order Pint No. 4, thus indicating it was a very early stage of the evening. There was mutual recognition with Pete having the grace not to remind Stan about his earlier challenge, but in time, with Pete finishing off Pint No. 9, the reminder was issued.

'How about another go at that Yard of Ale?' suggested one of Stan's friends.

'No,' said Pete, shaking his head and

pretending to be uninterested. 'I'm no good at that sort of thing.'

'A fiver, then? Me and my mates will all put a quid into the kitty – you do the same. Winner takes all.'

'Go on, Pete,' shouted someone from the bar. 'Have a go … we'll help you pay the money if you have to.'

'You first,' Pete said to Stan. 'You show me again.'

'I'll do it against the clock this time,' Stan said. 'Stopwatches out, lads?' And so Pete rose to the challenge. Stan filled the Yard from the bar pumps, prepared for his feat by standing with his legs apart and his hands on the neck of the big glass and someone shouted 'Go!'

In one long smooth action, he sank the contents in nine seconds without spilling a drop. It was an impressive display and he handed the glass to Pete who in turn passed it to George. George filled it and said, 'This is on me, Pete, two and a half pints.'

And so Pete stood in the middle of the bar with the full Yard of Ale before him and at the word 'Go' he swung into action. He sank the entire contents in eight and a half seconds, performing the smoothest of operations with no spillage whatever, then handed the glass back to George and smacked his lips. 'Not a bad pint or two,' he commented. 'Not bad at all.'

Stan, the man from York, was gracious in defeat; he and his pals proffered their pound notes, but Pete said, 'Stick it in the Lifeboat Box.'

The regulars of the Hopbind realized that Pete now had a new skill. He could down a Yard of Ale in little more time than it took a town-bred champion to do likewise but it transpired he could only do so after drinking nine pints in advance, something to do with lubricating his throat, he claimed, and preparing his stomach for a rapid intake. It was a few days after his triumph that I discovered his new name. No longer was he Twelve-pint Pete – now he was Yard of Ale Yardley and I heard that he was practising hard to become champion of Yorkshire, or even the world. I could envisage the billing on local posters if he ever decided to perform or demonstrate his art on a wider scale – Yard of Ale Yardley from Yorkshire.

That same village pub was the regular haunt of another character who set himself a daily challenge. His name was Sylvester Galbraith and he was a seventy-year-old retired forestry worker who lived in Gate Cottage, among conifers at the east entrance to Craydale Estate. In times past, the cottage had been one of the gatehouses to the estate, but now that that particular entrance was rarely used, the cottage was not required for a gatekeeper. Instead, it was rented by the estate to anyone who might wish to use it – and so Sylvester and his wife had rented it. They had been there since his retirement some five years earlier, both of them ekeing out their pensions with occasional work at Craydale House – bits of gardening, house work, helping at social functions and so forth. Although the cottage was very remote, being half a mile from Craydale House, a mile from Craydale village and some two and a half miles from Elsinby, the Galbraiths loved the place.

I popped in from time to time, chiefly to ask if they'd noticed any villainous folks around like poachers, burglars, house-breakers, litter dumpers and their ilk, but also to ensure the couple were not in need of medical assistance or help of any kind. After all, they were elderly and they lived alone, without a telephone, in a very beauti-ful but remote part of Yorkshire. They appreciated such spontaneous calls from me and, of course, from the passing district nurse, postman, milkman and various estate workers. Whenever we called, however unexpectedly, Fay Galbraith would always offer a cup of tea or coffee, generally with a biscuit or scone she had made. As I grew to know them, or more about them, I discovered a curious trait in Sylvester – he hated the notion of unnecessarily spending money on petrol for his Morris Minor. Having grown up with horses and having spent a lot of his time cycling to work in his younger days, the idea of propelling his car down any hill seemed quite ridiculous. Like his pedal cycle, it could freewheel down slopes and hills and in Sylvester's view, it *should* run down freely without any need for the engine to be running or the gears engaged. He utterly failed to see the sense in spending money on petrol which was consumed by driving down hills when they could be negotiated without any input from the engine. The fact that the engine and gears also served as an aid to braking did not occur to him and so, over the years, he had developed an astonishing knowledge of all the hills in the area, identifying all those down which he could take his car without using the engine. He would switch off the ignition at the summit and coast downwards with the wind whistling around his paint-work and with never a drop of petrol being used unnecessarily.

In his travels around the county, he knew precisely where he could switch off his engine and disengage his gears to achieve the longest possible run – one of his favourites was the wonderful flowing descent of Skelder which provides a run of almost five miles from Egton Moor into Whitby along the A171. Sylvester would switch off his engine as he crested the summit above Egton Low Moor and sail splendidly down towards Whitby without using a drop of petrol until he arrived at the outskirts of the town. The A169 provides a similar exhilarating freewheel run from Sleights Moor above Goathland – this is a three-mile joy which takes you down Blue Bank into Sleights, while the A170 offers similar unbridled happiness on the run from Tom Smiths Cross into Helmsley when approaching from Sutton Bank. This is another delight of some four petrol-saving miles and Sylvester would often take that route to save himself a few shillings' worth of fuel. There are many similar long descents both in the North York Moors and in the Yorkshire Dales, but in the area around Ashfordly and Aidensfield there were others, perhaps not so long and perhaps just a little steeper in places, but Sylvester knew them all. Even if it meant a run of a few hundred yards without consuming his precious petrol, he would take advantage of it.

From time to time, I have been asked whether this practice is illegal and I could never produce a completely satisfactory answer, other than to say it could be argued that full control of the vehicle might be jeopardized by switching off the engine and disengaging the gears. There might have been some offence under the old Highways Acts, such as driving a carriage so as to endanger life or limb. In that case, a motor car might be considered a carriage but in any case, it might be argued that disengaging the gears and engine, and freewheeling down a hill is tantamount to driving without reasonable consideration for other road users – in such cases, the person behind the wheel is 'driving' even though the engine is switched off. Whatever the legal situation at the time, I had never come across anyone who had been prosecuted, usually because no accidents occurred during those freewheel runs. I felt that, in a last resort, I might consider an offence under Section 35 of the Offences Against the Person Act of 1861. That created the offence of 'Any person having the charge of any carriage or vehicle, by wanton or furious driving, or racing, or other wilful misconduct, or by wilful neglect, doing or causing to be done any bodily harm to any person'. That could only be utilized, of course, if anyone was hurt – including the driver!

What it all means, however, is that there was no specific law to forbid the actions of such freewheelers, and so Sylvester could flow down as many hills as he wished. As it happened, one of those long hills led, quite literally, from outside his front door right down to the village of Elsinby. However, the road levelled out before reaching the Hopbind Inn and when Sylvester wanted to go to the Hopbind for a drink, he always tried to freewheel from his own doorstep right to the front door of the pub. And he never quite succeeded. He reached the village, but always came to a halt about fifty yards from his destination, and that failure infuriated him. In time, his desire to coast to the very door of the pub became something of an obsession.

I learned of this when I popped into the Hopbind early one Friday evening on one of my official visits. The bar contained about ten regulars and when I entered, they were all standing at the windows and looking along the village street.

'Are you all expecting something?' I asked George Ward, the landlord.

'Just Sylvester,' he smiled. 'He's due about now.'

'So why the welcoming party?' I asked.

George then explained about Sylvester's freewheeling tactics and his deep desire to actually reach the front door of the pub without using his engine. 'He usually comes to a halt halfway between here and the church,' George told me. 'All it needs is for him to come up behind a slow driver or a tractor; if he has to brake, he loses his impetus and that slows him down a lot and means he doesn't get so far along the level stretch down here. The gradient means he can generally reach that point between me and the church, if he's not slowed down *en route*. The furthest he's got beyond that point is outside Jasmine Cottage, that's the one with the green door.'

'So why the reception party?' I asked.

'Well, when we discovered what he was

doing, we said we'd buy him free drinks for a month if he ever managed to reach the pub. He's a bit on the tight side, a sort of rustic Scrooge, and we want to be sure he doesn't try to deceive us. I mean, he could start his engine or get somebody to push him those final few yards, and that would be cheating.'

'You think he'll never cover the full distance?' I put to them.

'No,' said one of them. 'He's been trying for years without success. And we know why. If you look along the street, you can see it dips ever so slightly outside the church, and then rises almost imperceptibly. Sylvester can coast into that dip, most times he does the run in fact, but he never has enough speed to get him over that little rise. It's the shallowest of crests, you never notice it when you're walking or driving a car, but when you're freewheeling, or trying to push-start someone's car, then you know it's there.'

Now that they had mentioned that tiny incline in the main street, I could see it as I stared along the road – what I had always regarded as a level stretch of highway was, in fact, very slightly undulating, but it was enough to frustrate Sylvester at the end of his regular run. And as we stood and stared, Sylvester's Morris Minor hove into view, coasting along at some four or five miles an hour until it came slowly to a halt at its usual place – almost opposite the church. He had failed again. Like hawks, his observers kept their eyes open for tell-tale signs of exhaust fumes being emitted, and they strained their ears for sounds of his engine being started – and sure enough, Sylvester fired his engine to carry his car for the final fifty yards.

He drove into the car-park and moments later was in the pub. 'I will do it,' he told his mates. 'One of these days, I'll get here. If I dare just to take that top corner a bit wider without touching my brakes, I could gain a bit extra speed to get me over that last bit, but I daren't swing out in case summat's coming the other way...'

I left him to his sorrows as I continued my patrol and in the days and weeks that followed I saw Sylvester coasting along in his silent car, rocking himself backwards and forwards in the driving seat in the manner of a cart driver helping his horse by producing some on-board momentum. I must admit I once tried to emulate his run – passing his house on a quiet morning, I switched off the engine of my Mini-van and allowed it to coast down the road towards Eltering. As I approached the corner which he wanted to take in a wide arc, I felt myself touch the brakes just a fraction so that I could safely negotiate the bend – and I could see now that if I was able to venture to the wrong side of the road to gain a wider sweep, I could have maintained my speed and that might just get me to the Hopbind Inn without the engine. But I didn't make it. Like Sylvester, I came to a halt near the church – there was just not enough momentum to get me over that tiniest of crests.

I forgot about Sylvester and his mission, but one autumn morning, I was patrolling through Elsinby and discovered that either a spring or a burst water main had erupted through the tarmac road surface almost opposite the church. Water was gushing forth and happily it flowed easily into the pretty beck which flows along the side of the road, but clearly it needed immediate attention. I radioed Ashfordly Police Station with a request that they contact the county council so that urgent work could begin, and within a couple of hours, workmen arrived to dig up the road and repair the burst. It was not a spring – it was a water main which had fractured and within a day, it had been repaired. It meant that the road at that point would require resurfacing and so that task would follow.

In time, the new surface was laid and all signs of the repair were covered with a new layer of tarmacadam – but it had an unexpected bonus for Sylvester. The short length of road outside the church was now raised by a couple of inches or so – and that evening, Sylvester coasted along it, now able to surmount the hitherto unconquerable summit outside Jasmine Cottage so that he could reach the Hopbind Inn all the way from his home without once using his engine.

The question now was whether the other regulars should buy him free drinks on each occasion he achieved that long-desired objective, or whether once was enough. I felt it was not a matter for the police.

Chapter Five

In common with the priest, vicar, doctor, squire or any other prominent person in a small village, it was inevitable during my time at Aidensfield that I, as the local constable, would be a constant focus of interest. That fascination extended to everything I did, but more unsettling was the fact it included my wife and children – and also friends and relations who visited our hilltop police house. Villagers knew when we bought a different car, went on holiday, had visitors for tea, changed our curtains or wallpapered the living-room; they knew if the cat died, whether my parents were staying for the weekend, whether my lawn needed a trim or my patch of vegetables contained rather more weeds than was deemed acceptable. I often wondered if they scrutinized our washing-line or waste-bin to study the more personal aspects of our life.

Although that kind of intense personal interest from others can be rather unsettling, especially to those unaccustomed to it, it is seldom malicious. In our case, it was little more than a very overt way of showing instinctive interest in the activities of another person and there were times when such nosiness could be beneficial. I'd be told if old Mrs Blenkinsop hadn't been seen for a few days, or if lame Mr Briggs hadn't taken his milk in, or whether the couple next to the post office had left their curtains closed all day. This kind of village gossip can sometimes be a life-saver because it can alert the authorities to those in need, and although townspeople who came to live in villages like Aidensfield could find it very unsettling, we village folk regarded it a perfectly normal part of our daily existence.

In time, everyone who lives in a small village community grows accustomed to the fact that others know all about them and their daily routine – after all, the person who is the focus of such interest generally knows all about other people too! It is far better to tolerate this kind of interest than there to be no interest at all – and I write these words having just read of an elderly gentleman who lay dead in his town house for three years without anyone realizing. That kind of indifference could and would never happen in a Yorkshire village – although I can't speak for our southern counterparts!

Having grown accustomed to this kind of fascination by others for the trivia of one's own life, however, it must be said that there are times it can create problems and on one occasion I was faced with such a dilemma. Before relating the series of incidents which led to my embarrassment, I should make it clear that I now realize I should have known better than to embark upon the events which led to it. But all that is in hindsight – at the time I thought that what I was doing was acceptable because I was doing it in full sight of the village and its occupants. But I hadn't bargained for the sheer power of gossip and innuendo – all because I gave driving lessons to a very pretty young woman.

Like all police officers who have to drive official vehicles as part of our duty, we had to qualify by passing a police driving test, the standard of which was comparable to the civilian advanced driver's examination. In my case, I was qualified to the high police standards, for driving motor cycles, motor cars and personnel carriers with a capacity of up to twelve persons.

There were occasions when I had to drive vehicles of any of these categories as part of my duty and like all police officers, I took a pride in my driving. Much of that professional pride and care was due to the fact that if I was involved in a traffic accident while driving a police vehicle, then I might not be allowed to drive one again – unless I passed a subsequent test. I'd be grounded, to put it in the jargon of RAF pilots. Such pressures made us drive very carefully and very well, both on and off duty, and it was widely considered among the public that a fully trained police driver was an expert in his craft. And that is why Marion Appleyard asked me to teach her to drive. Or rather, she asked Mary, my wife, if I would teach her.

Marion was a good friend of Mary's; our children went to the same school and played together, we visited one another's homes and Mary and Marion were very close indeed. I was similarly friendly with Marion's husband, Keith, although being a policeman meant that I could never be very close to anyone – and especially to Keith because he was a self-employed professional driving instructor. He lived in Aidensfield and operated a single vehicle for his tuition. I had always to be aware that one of his pupils might breach the road traffic laws and that meant I mustn't exercise favours towards Keith or any of his pupils. I had to treat everyone with fairness – without fear or favour, as the term goes. Nonetheless, Keith and I were as friendly towards one another as any policeman and driving instructor could be. It was Mary, therefore, who put the proposal to me one evening after work.

'Why does she want me to teach her?' was the obvious question in my mind. 'Keith's a driving instructor, surely he should teach her.'

'He can't,' Mary laughed. 'He can't teach Marion.'

'Why?' I puzzled. 'Is it against some code of practice? I don't know of any reason why he can't teach his own wife.'

'No, it's not that. He's tried, and she's tried. He's given her lessons and she's tried to listen to him and do as he says ... but they fall out. She said that after only a few minutes in the car with Keith, she gets to screaming pitch, he loses his temper and they have an almighty row. Then they come home early without her learning anything. She's been trying for years now and still can't drive, poor Marion. And more than once, she's asked Keith to stop the car and let her out, and she's caught the bus home.

It just doesn't work, Nick. She's given up asking him now, but she wants to learn to drive. And he's the only professional instructor around here.'

'So what makes you think I can teach her? She might be impossible ... if Keith can't cope, why does she think I can? Perhaps she's a bundle of nerves; maybe she's incapable of co-ordinating her movements when she's behind the wheel, or is she one of those unteachable people?'

'She's none of those, Nick, she's very nice and capable, and she's always calm and cheerful – until she gets behind a steering wheel with Keith in charge.'

'All right, but why me?'

'It was my idea. She really does want to learn and you taught me to drive, remember? You were patient with me and used your police driving knowledge to prepare me for my test.'

'Yes, but we weren't married then. If we had been, we might have fallen out and argued and got upset...'

'But we didn't, Nick; you're a calm person, you'd be able to teach Marion without any trouble. I know you would. And if it doesn't work out, or if she is unteachable, you can always stop the lessons.'

'It would have to be in my off-duty time in a private car, that goes without saying, and I can't accept any money from her,' I reminded Mary. 'It would have to be done as if she was a friend...'

'She is a friend, Nick, she's my friend.'

'So what's Keith think about all this?' was my next concern.

'He doesn't know; she wants to surprise him,' Mary now told me. 'She'd like to learn without him knowing anything about it, as a surprise. She'll pay expenses – you know, petrol money and whatever – she'll even hire a car if we can't use ours. We talked it through, me and Marion. She said she wanted to ask you direct, but I said I'd act as intermediary, just to show I had no objection to you and her going off together.'

'There'll be talk in the village,' I heard myself say. 'You can't keep a thing like this a secret for long, and if I'm seen going for drives with Marion, it won't take long for the gossip to reach Keith's ears.'

'I realize that, and so does she. If there is a problem, I can cope, we both can,' Mary said with confidence. 'I'll tell Keith if I have to, or any of the gossips, that it was my idea. But if you're open in what you're doing and don't try to hide anything, there should be no problems.'

'So how does she propose to fit in these lessons, with Keith always on the road? He teaches his pupils on local roads, so it's almost a certainty we'd meet each other sooner or later.'

'She knows his programme and the routes he takes with his pupils. She knows where he does his hill-starts, three-point turns and so on. He always uses the same places and she can make sure you avoid him.'

'You've got it all worked out, haven't you?' I smiled.

'Well, it's important to Marion, really important, Nick, so we talked about it a lot. We've tried to anticipate the sort of problems that might arise ... but as I said, we're all going to be doing it in the open, so there should be no problems – apart from not letting Keith find out.'

'I'd be happier if he knew about it,' I put to her.

'I told Marion that's how you'd feel, but she wants it to be a surprise for him – she wants to suddenly get into their car and drive it as if she's been driving for years.'

'There's no need for her to hire a car,' I said, thinking of the expense. 'We can use ours; it is insured for other drivers, provided

I don't make a charge.'

'I said we could do that. You can't use theirs, Keith uses it all the time.'

And so, somewhat against my better judgement and with a slight feeling of apprehension, I agreed to teach Marion to drive. Mary would act as the go-between taking calls from Marion to suggest a time and place to collect her. The two ladies would have to work around my own irregular duty hours, and Marion would know Keith's timing and any route he would be using at a particular time. We would do everything possible to avoid that part of the countryside. I'd heard it said – probably wrongly – that ten or twelve hours thorough instruction could enable a reasonable pupil to reach test standard, whilst a further three hours or so, under mock-test conditions, complete with questions about the Highway Code, should enable the pupil to pass the driving test which prevailed at that time.

It was two o'clock on the following Tuesday afternoon, a beautiful sunny June day, that Marion arrived at the police house on foot, carrying a bag which contained a pair of L plates and looking absolutely beautiful. She was infinitely more attractive than I had realized – a tall, slim, dark-haired

126

woman in her mid-thirties. Her skin was tanned and she had slender legs that seemed endless as they left the confines of her pleated white mini-skirt. She wore light sandshoes, no stockings and a bright red blouse. Her face was divine, her dark eyes soft and gentle, and because the day was hot and sunny, she sported a pair of large sunglasses. Under normal circumstances, Mary would have been most unhappy if I'd announced I was taking this vision of loveliness for driving lessons in the rich, green countryside, but because the entire scheme was a joint initiative between Mary and Marion, they were happy to go along with it, and so was I.

As I tied the L plates to the front and rear bumpers of my car, Mary and Marion chatted and then we were ready. I had decided to take her towards Brantsford, partly because I knew the rural lanes would be very quiet, and partly because there was an old airfield at Stovensby which was ideal as a safe, traffic-free place for very early learner drivers. Before settling Marion in the driving seat, however, I asked about her previous driving experiences and it seemed Keith, in spite of the tensions that always developed between them, had managed to impart a good deal of rudimentary know-ledge. She could start the engine, make the car proceed in a straight line, change gear up and down, use the brakes and check her mirror. She lacked the more complicated skills like coping with reversing, hill starts, emergency braking, three-point turns, traffic lights, town traffic, pedestrian crossings and dual carriageways, but I was pleased we could dispense with the basic preliminaries.

Armed with this knowledge, therefore, I decided I could place her in the driving seat from the beginning and so we began our first lesson. Her eyes were alive with happi-ness as I said I would take her along the lanes, passing through Crampton, Lower Keld and Stovensby before arriving at the old airfield. By adopting that route, I told her, she'd have to cope with a few hills and a small amount of traffic in those villages, and then on the deserted old airfield, I could introduce her to emergency halts, three-point turns, the technique of reversing and, eventually, a spot of high-speed car control.

On that first outing, I realized that her skills were rather more limited than I anticipated – her theoretical knowledge was not supported by the necessary practice, but she was a quick learner and an intelligent driver. She made very rapid progress and by the end of our second lesson, a week later, I felt she was ready to tackle the traffic in Brantsford – especially as it was market-day and the place would be bustling with stalls, vehicles and pedestrians. On that occasion, I began her lesson with some complex drives through the villages, like reversing into cul-de-sacs, coping with tractors and agricultural machinery, avoiding dogs and pedestrians and looking out for delivery vans. This was followed by a session of emergency braking, three-point turns, reversing into a limited space and cornering sharply on the old airfield – all important elements in handling a moving car. And she coped admirably. There was no doubt she was ready to tackle Brantsford even if it was one of its busiest days. I allowed half an hour for that visit. I thought it would be enough stress for her first session in heavy traffic. But her response was always positive and eager, and I must admit I wondered why Keith had been unable to teach her these skills because she seemed eminently educable with a burning desire to be tutored.

Our rapid journey through Brantsford market-place went without much of a hitch, although there were a few heart-stopping moments as pedestrians sought to cross the street without checking for oncoming traffic, dogs ran about the road and produce vans moved in and out of parking places as if nothing else was there. If Marion learned anything by that experience, it was how to put the car's audible warning instrument to good use!

I was very impressed to see that, without losing her nerve, she guided the car between all the sudden hazards and fast-moving obstacles which were presented to her. I began to feel she was a natural driver and wondered if Keith had treated her as a brainless nincompoop, perhaps being unable – or unwilling – to recognize her natural talent. And so, in subsequent lessons, I began to test her skills in more difficult places – coping with hills and sharp corners, hill starts, difficult reversing movements, driving through busy towns with pedestrian crossings, schools, roundabouts and traffic lights. With her knowledge of Keith's daily routine, we avoided him by visiting neighbouring towns – I took her to Scarborough on one occasion so that she could cope with a packed seaside town and crowds of jaywalking tourists. I took her out at night to learn how to drive in the dark. We did umpteen hill starts on the notorious gradients of the North York Moors and countless three-point turns in busy streets, visiting market towns like Malton, Pickering, Whitby, Brantsford, Eltering and Galtreford, but always managing to avoid Ashfordly and Keith. And after each outing, I provided Mary with a full account of the trip and an appraisal of Marion's progress.

But as our lessons progressed, I began to notice that barbed jibes began to surface. One farmer said, 'Saw you in Galtreford last market-day with that woman, Constable … not your wife, I know. A nice looker…'

'I'm teaching her to drive,' I explained.

'Aye, and I'm King Richard III! Tell us another!' he laughed.

A lady, anxious to determine whether or not I was having an affair, said, 'I hope things are all right between you and Mrs Rhea, Constable.'

'Yes, they're fine,' I said. 'We've no problems.'

'I am so pleased to hear that, it's just that my husband saw you with Mrs Appleyard in Malton one night, outside the Green Man

Hotel, alone in your car, he said...'

'I'm teaching Mrs Appleyard to drive.'

Other probing questions began to manifest themselves and each time I said I was teaching Marion to drive, I realized that such truthful statements were seldom accepted. It began to appear as if I was making a very weak excuse for meeting another woman, and I wondered whether I should have said to my critics, 'Yes, we're having a mad, passionate affair and we're considering running away with each other to live in bliss on some tropical island...'

Over the few weeks I taught Marion, that kind of barb became more prevalent and it was clear that the eyes of Aidensfield and district's gossips were now firmly focused on me and my new interest. I decided it might be wise to spend time in Aidensfield village centre with Marion, making a great point of showing how we were practising three-point turns, emergency-halts, reversing manoeuvres and hill starts. Then I realized that if I did that, it might seem as if I was desperately trying to cover up some underhand behaviour. Whatever I did to persuade the gossips that Marion and I were not doing anything wrong, our activities would never be seen in their true light.

I decided that the only real course of action was to continue as before, ignoring the misinterpretations that were inevitable. Then I received a telephone call from Sergeant Craddock.

'Ah, PC Rhea, glad I've caught you. Can you be in my office tomorrow morning at ten?'

'Yes, Sergeant,' I said in all innocence. 'Is there anything I should prepare? Returns? Statements? That outstanding accident file?'

'No,' he said sharply. 'Just be there.'

'Very good, Sergeant,' I said, wondering what was in store for me. His voice did not sound very welcoming; I guessed I was in some kind of trouble. It was with some trepidation that I motored to Ashfordly the following morning, making sure my uniform was brushed and my boots were polished. I arrived at the police station in good time, parked and went in. Alf Ventress was installed at his desk amid a galaxy of unwashed coffee mugs which stood like sentinels beneath a cloud of cigarette smoke and among a carpet of bread crumbs. He looked up in some surprise at my arrival.

''Morning, Alf.' I greeted him in as jaunty a manner as I could muster.

'Hello, Nick.' He produced a narrow

smile. 'I didn't expect to see you this early.'

'I've got to see Sergeant Craddock at ten,' I said.

'I'd make a coffee for you, but you've not got time to drink it.' He glanced at the clock. It was five to ten. 'He's in his office now, if you want to get it over with.'

'What's it all about?' I asked, gesturing with my hands to show I had no idea why I had been summoned to the regal presence.

'Search me,' he muttered. 'You're not being posted, are you?'

'Posted?' I must have sounded horrified at the prospect of being moved from Aidensfield – I was just getting settled in.

'Well, what else is there? Promoted?'

'Not me,' I said. 'I've not enough operational experience to get myself promoted. Craddock sounded angry when he rang.'

'Oh, dear, then it's a hot-water job, is it? You're up to the neck in something, are you?'

'I haven't a clue,' I confirmed, and then Sergeant Craddock's office door opened.

'Ah, PC Rhea, you'd better come in.'

He stalked back into his office and I followed like a poodle, standing before his desk as he settled into his chair. He studied me for a few seconds, as if assessing the state of my uniform and my general demeanour, and then, leaving me standing, said, 'You will be wondering why I have called you in this morning, PC Rhea?'

'Yes, I am, Sergeant, I have no idea.'

'I find this somewhat difficult, PC Rhea, but it has come to my notice, via Divisional Headquarters, that some disturbing rumours have been circulating of late, about you.'

'Me?' I was surprised. 'Why? What am I supposed to have done?'

He paused, licked his lips, and said, 'How are things at home? You know, between you and your wife?'

'Fine,' I said.

'You have a family, I believe? Children?'

'Yes, four,' I confirmed.

'It would be a dreadful shame if you did anything which would jeopardize your marriage – or indeed your career – would it not?'

'It would, and I would never do anything which would harm my family,' I assured him.

'Not even spend time alone with another woman? A very attractive young lady?'

'Ah, Mrs Appleyard,' I said. 'You're talking about Marion Appleyard?'

'Then you do know what I am talking about? And why you are here?'

'No, Sergeant, I have no idea what you are suggesting or why I have been brought here, although I might guess what the rumour-mongers are implying. The truth is that I am giving driving lessons to Mrs Appleyard, in my own time and at no cost to her other than helping with the petrol we use.'

'Ah. Driving lessons. I understand that her husband is a driving instructor, and a very capable one too.'

'Yes, he is, Sergeant.'

'And does he know about this, er, arrangement?'

'You are well informed, but no, his wife wants to keep it a secret.'

'Ah!'

'Sergeant, there is nothing sinister in all this. I am not having an affair, if that's what the rumours are suggesting. There is nothing between Mrs Appleyard and myself, other than the fact she's a very good friend of my wife.'

'So you are taking this woman out for drives in your own private car, alone, visiting places like Scarborough, Whitby and the moors, all well away from Ashfordly and Aidensfield, without anyone else present, and without the knowledge of her husband.'

'You make it sound dreadful, Sergeant!' I found my temper was rising. Normally, I am a very calm person, but the thought of being wrongfully accused of something, especially something which arose due to nothing more than rumour and innuendo, was enough to ruffle my proverbial feathers. 'Look' – my voice was rising now – 'I am taking her out for driving lessons, it's nothing more than that. It's in my own time; the car is insured; I am not being paid; I'm not moonlighting, or doing anything illegal or immoral.'

'You are aware of the provisions of the discipline code?' he put to me.

'Discipline code?' I almost shouted. 'There's nothing to say I can't teach a friend to drive!'

'But there is something which says a police officer commits a disciplinary offence if he acts in a manner which is likely to bring discredit to the reputation of the force.'

I took a deep breath. 'Sergeant, I am teaching a friend to drive, that's all. My wife suggested I do this to help her friend. Her husband cannot teach her, both she and her husband lose their tempers whenever he tries to teach her. They get nowhere with the lessons and so Mrs Appleyard asked my wife to ask me if I could help. She wants to learn to drive and to pass her driving test as a surprise to her husband. My wife makes all the arrangements so that we can co-ordinate our meetings, and keep away from Keith Appleyard. What else can I say? If you don't believe me, then I am quite happy for you to speak to my wife. I have nothing to hide, Sergeant. How on earth can teaching a friend to drive be regarded as likely to bring discredit to the police service?'

'In our work, PC Rhea, we must be seen to be above criticism, both in our official lives and in our private lives. A married constable, especially one who is in a position of extra trust as you are in your role as the constable of Aidensfield, and who is openly enjoying the company of a woman who is not his wife, may be regarded as doing something which could bring discredit to the service.'

'I can understand that, up to a point, if I was misbehaving but I am not, Sergeant, I am teaching a friend to drive. Nothing more.'

'But you must always consider the effect of your actions, PC Rhea. Even if you are behaving honourably, it can appear outwardly that you are not. The public perception of your activities may be quite different from the reality.'

'Are you telling me to stop these lessons, Sergeant?' I put to him. 'Or has that order come down from on high somewhere?'

'No, if you are merely giving lessons...'

'I *am* merely giving lessons,' I affirmed. 'There is no "if" about it.'

'Well, clearly, I cannot prevent you giving free driving lessons to a friend but if you were having an affair...'

'Sergeant, you said "if" again. Look, giving a lesson is all that I am doing. A driving lesson. All these ifs and buts and doubts are not part of this scenario. I am giving driving lessons to a friend who happens to be an attractive woman. I am not having an affair with her and have no intention of doing so, and if she wants to surprise her husband by passing her test, that is for her to decide.'

'I can understand that, but you know what happens to a village constable who does have an affair. The first step is to remove him from temptation, post him to a new police station a long way from the other woman.'

'Sergeant,' I went on, 'I have no idea who has asked you to speak to me like this, but you can tell whoever it is that I shall continue to give those lessons. Why should I give up if I am not doing anything wrong? And do you now think I will be removed from Aidensfield, for helping a friend? I hope we are not becoming like the KGB, spying on innocent people. It's getting like Franz Kafka's book, *The Trial*...'

'Good heavens, no, you must not think like that, PC Rhea, we are a million miles from behaving like the secret police.'

'No we're not!' I burst out. 'You, or someone in authority over you, is behaving just like the secret police, trying to stop me from behaving in a normal manner. What is wrong with what I am doing?'

'There is nothing wrong in teaching a friend to drive but–'

'There you go again, another "but", another piece of doubt! If this story reached the newspapers, Sergeant, they'd crucify you and those above you...'

'You wouldn't tell the papers, PC Rhea! That would be a disciplinary offence!'

'Not if my wife, or her friend told them,' I smiled. 'There are more ways of killing a cat...'

'Look.' He adopted a calmer note now. 'I was instructed to advise you on your private life, in view of serious rumours which have recently been circulating … I shall now report there is no justification for those rumours. But I must advise you to be very careful how you portray yourself in the eyes of the public. You must remember that your supervisory officers are out and about too, in civilian clothes, seeing things and making interpretations.'

'But surely, Sergeant, the truth must prevail? The truth never hurt anyone, did it? And what have I done that is wrong or illegal or immoral? Nothing. Tell that to your bosses, please.'

'I haven't done a very good job with this, have I?'

'Someone has listened to those rumours, Sergeant, and believed them. Or even set them off! I thought police officers were supposed to assess the evidence before taking action against a suspect? Unless it's one of their own officers, it seems. Then you can believe what you want!'

'PC Rhea, it is not in my nature to give apologies for what I believed, at the time, to be the right thing to do, but it is now clear that I have been swept along with the others, on a tide of mistrust. I am pleased you have listened to what I had to say, and that you have given me your version of events. I shall not speak to your wife, there is no need, nor shall I talk to Mrs Appleyard or her husband. I would add, though, that I wish to give you a friendly warning – by seeing this lady alone, as you have been doing, provides the perfect ingredients for malicious rumours. I know you realize that. What action you now take is your responsibility. I will report accordingly to Divisional Headquarters. And I do hope Mrs Appleyard passes her driving test.'

I went home in something of a daze and with a good deal of anger seething in my breast. When I talked it over with Mary, she suggested she could accompany me and Marion, but that would complicate matters if only because babysitters would then be required for our four children. As it happened, Marion had almost reached the stage of applying for her driving test so I encouraged her to make the necessary application – that would concentrate her mind, and now she would have to drive around the test course, familiarize herself with the Highway Code and attune herself to the stress of taking a test. I reckoned it meant three or four more lessons at the most and so I was prepared to let myself be seen by the rumour-mongers – I almost felt as if I should give them something to talk about!

It is not necessary to dwell any further on the matter, save to say that I completed the course with Marion, proof that she was a most capable driver.

When the day of her test arrived, we drove to the testing centre at Malton – Keith was busy with one of his pupils undergoing a similar test at Northallerton – and I allowed her to take the test in my car. It was an anxious wait – afterwards, I saw her drive into the parking area and sit in the car as the examiner confronted her with his sheet of paper containing his assessment. They sat for a long time and I thought he was pointing out her multifarious errors, so I hovered in the background until it was all over. But the examiner opened the door full of smiles, shook her by the hand and said, 'Congratulations', having presented her with her pass certificate.

I hurried to my car and was in time to see Marion sitting in the driving seat with tears streaming down her face, but they were tears of joy and happiness. I could see the pass certificate in her hands so I went to the front and rear bumpers, cut off the L plates with my pen-knife and entered the passenger seat, intending to give them to her as souvenirs.

But as I sat down and said, 'You drive us home,' she hurled herself across the seat, flung her arms round my neck and planted a massive wet and sloppy kiss on my lips. During that one moment of passion between us, all I could see through the window at the rear of my car was my superintendent. He was watching us – by chance, his daughter was also taking her test.

Hurriedly, I opened the car door, rushed out towards him and said, 'She's passed, sir, she's passed.'

'I did rather guess that, PC Rhea,' he smiled. 'Well done.'

It would be a fortnight later when my doorbell rang and I saw a somewhat effeminate young man standing there. I knew him; he lived in Aidensfield and was always rejected by his peers. Tony, in his mid-twenties, was a loner, a sad case really, but when I opened the door, he simpered, 'Mr Rhea, I heard about your success with Mrs Appleyard, the driving test you know, and I wondered if you would like to teach me...'

'I'm afraid I can't,' I had to tell him. 'My bosses have said I must do no more.'

Chapter Six

If things were not quite what they seemed whilst I was providing driving lessons for Marion Appleyard, a similar puzzle was provided by the sighting of a dark-skinned man wearing a turban and what appeared to be robes of the type worn by an Arab. The first sighting, on a brilliantly sunny Saturday morning in May, was by a pair of schoolboys who were exploring Aidensfield Wood in the hope of finding Robin Hood's Cave. Each of the lads was twelve years old and quite sensible, not given to making up false or exaggerated stories about their adventures, and both told their respective parents the same tale about seeing the Arab in Aidensfield Wood.

None of the parents thought anything more of the incident; certainly, it never occurred to them that it might be anything sinister, both sets of parents thinking it might have been a slight figment of a child's imagination, or perhaps a hiker or rambler dressed up in a very individual style of clothing. I heard about it from one of the parents, Phil Ramsey. Phil, in his mid-thirties, worked for a local plumber and by chance, he was chatting to Oscar Blaketon in the post office when I entered. He was telling Blaketon (my former sergeant) about the sighting and upon seeing me, Oscar said, 'Ah, Phil, this is just the chap! Tell him about the Arab.'

'Oh, well, I'm not complaining; I don't want him arrested or anything, there's no need for a fuss. He didn't approach the lads; he didn't even speak to them.'

'So what's it all about?' I asked.

Phil then told me about his son, Jamie, who had been exploring with his pal, Martin Godfrey.

When they were about mid-way along the path through Aidensfield Wood, they spotted the man among the trees. Both lads told the same story. The man had dark skin, almost black, and he wore the long flowing robes of an Arab, creamy-white in colour and a head covering of some kind which seemed to be secured upon his head with a rope-like ring. He was rushing along a minor path some distance from the main route and after a minute or so, the lads lost sight of him among the dense, freshly foliated trees. Each confirmed they had not been approached by the fellow, nor had they even been frightened – they were simply curious as to who he was or where he had come from. They had never seen him before and he was quite alone.

After listening to this yarn, I told Phil I'd had no reports of anyone answering that description being spotted in the locality, nor had I received reports of anyone missing from home, or from an institution of any kind.

'How about Maddleskirk Abbey?' I asked. 'Could it have been one of the monks?'

'I thought about that,' nodded Phil, 'but Jamie goes to the Catholic school and he knows what a monk looks like. Besides, those monks are Benedictines, they wear black robes.'

'A visiting cleric of some kind?' suggested Blaketon. 'Exploring the Yorkshire country-side?'

'It's possible,' I said. 'The Abbey attracts visitors from around the world, from all religious persuasions. I think the most likely explanation is that it was a priest or a monk of some sort, enjoying a short break from the monastic routine!'

And we left it at that. Having listened to

Phil, I tended to agree that it could have been a visiting monk dressed in the robes of an obscure order, but as the fellow had not done anything to warrant questions from me, I allowed the incident to slide to the back of my mind. It would be about a week later, when Dick Crossley, a gamekeeper on Ashfordly Estate, hailed me as I patrolled through Elsinby.

'Ah, Nick, glad I caught you. There was a queer chap in one of our woods the other day; I thought I'd better mention it.'

'Queer? Poaching, was he?' That was my first instinctive response.

'No, he wasn't doing anything wrong, in fact he was using a public footpath which passes through that wood – Elsinby Plantation – but I thought I'd better mention it. I thought he looked as if he was in a hurry.'

'Why, Dick? Why mention it if he was not doing anything wrong? You said he was queer, so what was he doing?'

'He was an Arab, Nick, with a black face and those long white robes, rushing through the wood all alone. I've checked locally, at holiday cottages and so on, but there's no one like that staying hereabouts. I just thought you ought to know.'

'Thanks.' And then I told him of the

similar sighting in Aidensfield Wood, adding the possibility that it might have been a monk who'd been visiting Maddleskirk Abbey. Dick had not considered that possibility and the notion seemed to satisfy him – he reckoned a wandering monk was not a threat to his pheasants and partridges.

A few days later, I had reason to visit Maddleskirk Abbey as part of my duties. I had to check the credentials of some Europeans, whom we termed aliens, who worked there temporarily as domestic staff, and during my discussions with the prior, I decided to mention the galloping Arab. I had no official reason to pursue that enquiry, but merely wanted to satisfy my own curiosity.

'We've no one here who answers that description, Mr Rhea,' he assured me. 'The only visitors we've had recently were six Franciscans and two Buddhists, neither of whose members dress like Arabs. The Franciscans wear dark-brown robes, as you know, and those particular Buddhist monks wore saffron-coloured robes.'

In further attempts to find an answer to the puzzling sightings, I asked around the village, paying particular attention to people who lived in remote places, or who were regular visitors to the woodlands, moors, riverbanks and network of rural footpaths. But, to my knowledge, no one else had seen the galloping Arab. In the absence of further sightings, the matter receded in my mind once again and in time I persuaded myself it must have been a visiting monk or priest whose unfamiliar garments had created an unclear image in the minds of the witnesses.

And then a party of mums and young children saw an American Indian. It was a scorching hot day in August and a party of young mums from Aidensfield – nine or ten of them – had gone down to the river with their families. In addition to the adults, there would be some twenty children aged between five and ten. It was a very shallow place with a sandy bed and wide shore; the water moved slowly over the riverbed and it was considered a very safe place for children to swim and paddle.

Within easy access of Aidensfield, it attracted parents who had small children, particularly during the school's summer holidays when the weather was hot and dry. Lots of them would venture down to the riverside with picnics and so it was on that hot August Wednesday afternoon. It was Wendy Carstairs who told me about it.

'I'm not complaining, Nick,' was her opening remark. 'He did nothing wrong, nothing at all, but just ran along the path right behind us.'

'An American Indian?' I sought confirmation of this.

'Yes, he wore a full headdress with feathers, but his chest and torso were bare and he had long khaki trousers with feathered legs, and moccasins on his feet. I remember the moccasins because they looked so comfortable and didn't make a sound as he ran. I thought they were rather like carpet slippers.'

'And what colour was his skin?'

'Oh, red, like copper,' she said. 'A lovely tan colour, all down his back, and his face, too, but his face had war paint on; red, green and white streaks I think, and some bits of blue. He was just like one of those Indians you see in films.'

'Was he carrying anything? A rifle? Bow and arrow? Tomahawk? Or making any kind of noise? War cries?' I smiled.

'No, nothing. I'm sure he wasn't carrying anything, no bag or bow and arrows, nothing like that. And there was no noise; we had no idea he was anywhere near us and I just happened to look up as he was

151

running past. I think he was just as surprised to see us, although to be honest, the children were making a lot of noise as they do. Maybe if he was running fast, he didn't realize they were so close by.'

'Perhaps he was just as surprised to see you?'

'I think he was; he just ran along the path behind the alder trees and continued without saying a word or even looking at us. Some of the children noticed him, then whooped and cried like Indians do when they dance around a camp-fire, but he took no notice of them and vanished. I never saw him come back.'

'And you say he was not a threat?'

'No, I'm sure he wasn't. I think he just wanted to get out of our sight...'

'Age? Any idea how old he was?'

'Well, judging by his running and his figure, I'd say he was a fairly young man, Nick. Late twenties perhaps, or early thirties. He was quite tall, about your height, and well built; he looked very fit and strong.'

I thanked Wendy for this information and promised I would maintain my interest in the American Indian, and I told her about the running Arab, too. To my knowledge, we had no Indian encampments or reservations within the district, nor did I know of any living amongst us, perhaps with a desire to return to their native customs from time to time. I wondered if it was possible that a man with American Indian origins was living in Aidensfield and decided that, once more, I would make discreet enquiries. But I discovered nothing.

No other reports of the galloping Indian came my way and, as before, the incident began to fade in my memory. That long, hot summer brought no more reports of similar incidents and so, as time passed, I forgot about the Arab and the Indian.

There was nothing to remind me – no reported attacks in the area, no sightings of people doing odd things, no piles of discarded clothes found, and consequently, those galloping characters were forgotten.

Then, one dark evening in early October, when I was patrolling in the Mini-van, I received a radio call from Alf Ventress who was staffing Ashfordly Police Station. 'Ah, Nick,' he said. 'I've just had a call from the ambulance service, there's been a traffic accident in the woods on Crampton Heights. Somebody's rung from a kiosk, there's an injury, not serious, although an ambulance is *en route*. Can you attend?'

'I'm on my way, Alf. I'll be there in five or six minutes.'

'Give us a sit.rep when you can,' he requested and then I was on my way, blazing through the dark lanes with my headlights on full beam and my blue light flashing as I made for Crampton Heights. I knew the area well. It was a popular picnic site and viewpoint above Crampton and the road through the area boasted extensive views to the south-east. The day time views were stunning, but, even at night, the expansive vista below with all the lights and dark mysterious horizons, was fascinating. There were parking places which attracted visitors both night and day.

Much of the hill top was covered with deciduous trees and if you drove from Crampton village towards the Heights, you drove up towards the summit through a double row of huge beeches which formed a beautiful and spectacular avenue at every season of the year. I think they had been planted many years earlier on the authority of Lord Crampton, the road then being part of the Crampton Estate. Behind the beeches were the extensive Crampton woodlands which were open to the public and very popular all the year around. They attracted masses of strollers and even more serious hikers, as well as dog-walkers, bird-watchers and the whole range of country visitors.

When I arrived, I found a couple of parked cars with their headlights shining on the scene of the accident, whose drivers had stopped to help, and an ambulance with its blue light flashing. As I drew to a halt, I saw a Ford Consul with its bonnet wrapped around one of the beeches and a casualty already being loaded into the vehicle on a stretcher. I parked nearby with my blue light flashing and hurried to make an assessment of the casualty's condition before he was whisked away. It was a man and he was conscious, and I soon established that apart from facial bruising, his only serious injury appeared to be a broken left arm. He was not in a critical condition and was able to converse with me, but the ambulanceman did not want to delay things as the casualty might be suffering from shock. In the time available, I managed to learn that he was David Andrews aged 47, a commercial traveller working for a frozen food company, and that he lived in Ashfordly. I assured him I would inform his wife, but he asked me

155

not to. He said he'd telephone from the hospital as he'd rather do that himself than have a policeman knocking on her door at night. I established he'd been alone in the car, then obtained his address and told him I'd pop in to see him as soon as possible. Having allowed me a little time with the casualty, the ambulance departed for Ashfordly Hospital before I'd been able to establish precisely what had happened.

I turned to the two drivers who were standing by, but neither had witnessed the accident. They had no idea what had caused the man to swerve off the carriageway and hit the tree. Each had merely pulled up very soon afterwards to offer what assistance they could and one had driven into Crampton to call the emergency services from the telephone kiosk, but had then found someone else had already done so. As he'd returned to the scene, the ambulance had arrived. Both drivers said the casualty had been conscious and able to walk, even if he was in some pain, and surely suffering from shock.

I thanked them both and allowed them to leave. I was then left with a badly damaged car. It was completely off the road and thus not causing any kind of obstruction or danger. The tree was not damaged apart from some deep scratches and scrapes to the bark of its trunk and it was not at risk of collapsing. I took the necessary measurements of the scene, made a rough sketch plan for my report and concluded that, for some unknown reason, the car had swerved off the road to hit the tree. In the headlights of my own vehicle I could see there were tyre marks on the road to suggest it had been coming down the hill at the time; some short brake-marks confirmed that opinion. It seemed the car had not crossed the road but had swerved to its nearside and mounted the grass verge before coming to rest with the front of its bonnet crumpled against the very stout and solid tree-trunk.

No other car appeared to have been involved, none of the tyres had punctured suddenly and no one else was injured. It was a driver-only accident and injury, as we termed it. But why had this man swerved off the road?

Being a commercial traveller, he was probably a very good and safe driver; it was not particularly late at night so I doubted if he'd fallen asleep at the wheel, and while he was talking to me in the ambulance, I had not detected any sign of alcohol on his breath. But only he could tell me what had happened and I would have to wait a while for that. His medical treatment was more important than immediate completion of my accident report file. I removed some of his belongings from the car and secured it as best I could; it wouldn't go far without the help of a breakdown truck. When I got home, I'd ring a local garage and ask them to remove it as soon as possible, preferably tomorrow morning in daylight. I'd ask for the car to be removed to their own premises, and would inform Mr Andrews of its whereabouts; he could then liaise with the garage and his insurance company about its eventual disposal. After providing Alf Ventress with a situation report over my radio, I went home, rang the garage to arrange collection of the damaged car and booked off duty. Tomorrow, I would check with the hospital about Mr Andrews' condition and then arrange to interview him.

Shortly after nine the following morning, I rang Ashfordly Hospital to enquire after the condition of David Andrews and was told he had suffered severe bruising to his chest area along with a few cuts and bruises to his face, arms and legs, and a broken left arm.

His arm was the most serious of his injuries and it had been put in plaster. After spending the night in hospital, he would be allowed home that morning, but only after the consent of the ward doctor. His wife was expected to collect him around eleven.

I would not visit him in hospital, but decided to call at the house that afternoon, allowing time to settle in and come to terms with the accident. I rang in advance to make an appointment and so it was that at half past two, I was admitted to his smart semi-detached house in Ashfordly where his wife soon produced a cup of tea and biscuits as we chatted in his lounge. He looked rather battered about the face and his left arm was in a sling, but he sounded strong and cheerful. Being a commercial traveller, he knew the sort of thing I required in the aftermath of a traffic accident, such as his driving licence and certificate of insurance, and they were already waiting for me on a side table. After noting the relevant details, I turned to the accident.

'So, Mr Andrews,' I smiled. 'What happened?'

'I hadn't been drinking, you know. I was on my way home after a day working in the East Riding.'

'I believe you!' I smiled. 'So what happened?'

He shook his head as if still puzzled by the chain of events which had led to his crash. 'You're not going to believe this, Mr Rhea, and I'm not one for thinking I saw a ghost, but a cavalier ran out of those trees; right in front of me and galloped along the verge … I swerved instinctively, I thought he was coming across the road … it wasn't a ghost, Mr Rhea, I'm not given to seeing things like that. He was real enough.'

'A cavalier?' I puzzled. 'Not a car?'

'No, a man, a tall chap, running as if all the hounds in hell were chasing him. He shot out of those trees and my lights caught him. I thought he was coming right into my path so I swerved and hit that tree…'

'So where did he go?'

'He came to the driver's side and opened the door, saw me groaning or whatever I was doing, made me as comfortable as he could and said he'd ring for the ambulance. Then he just ran down the hill towards the village. I never saw him again.'

'So why do you describe him as a cavalier?'

'Well, it was the way he was dressed. He reminded me of that painting by Frans

Hals, *The Laughing Cavalier.* He had a lovely blue costume, very ornate with trimmings on it, a big, bulging sort of jerkin, and those wide trousers and a big hat with a huge brim on it with a feather sticking up, an ostrich feather by the look of it ... and he had a little black moustache and long curly hair, in ringlets...'

'You got a good look at him!'

'Not particularly, he wasn't in my sights for very long, but I had enough time to absorb most of the details ... I mean, it wasn't the most usual of things to be confronted with after an accident. I thought I was seeing a ghost at first, when he ran into the road that was, but when he came to the car and said he'd go for help, well, I realized he was real enough and had a fairly good look in spite of what had happened. I've no idea who he was, but he was no ghost.'

'And that was all?'

'It was. He ran off and left me nursing my arm. I sat in the passenger seat and then those two cars turned up. The ambulance was there in minutes and then you arrived.'

Mr Andrews could tell me little more about the accident, save to reassure me no other vehicle or person was involved and so, after inspecting his documents and listing all his injuries, I left. I felt sure there would be no question of prosecuting him for careless driving or any of the other driving offences and offered my condolences for his plight. Shortly afterwards, I checked with the supervisor of the telephone exchange in Ashfordly, and with Ashfordly Hospital's receptionist, but the man who had made that emergency call about the accident had not given his name or address. It had been requested by the hospital, but he'd declined, saying he was merely passing by. All that I could elicit was that the caller had been a man and he appeared to have a cultivated accent. That could include several men living in the district – and a lot who worked in the area. I knew of no criminal offence for which that running cavalier might be charged even if it could be proved he had caused the accident. There was an offence often known as jay walking, but that did not apply in this case. Jay walking was a term used when a pedestrian failed to comply with the directions given by a uniformed police officer engaged on traffic duty – the essential constituents of that offence were not present in the Crampton Heights case. Accordingly, when I submitted my accident report, I stated that Mr Andrews had been startled by a man who had suddenly appeared ahead of him, necessitating instant avoidance by Mr Andrews.

I did not mention that he had been dressed like a cavalier, otherwise I'd have been faced with allegations that Andrew had been drunk or thought he'd seen a ghost, so I merely recommended no further action against Mr Andrews. This was endorsed by Sergeant Craddock. It would be a few days later when he met me at a rendezvous point and commented on the case.

'Funny thing, that accident with that man in the woods,' he mused. 'You never did find out who he was, I suppose? The man who startled the car driver?'

'Not a clue, Sergeant,' I had to admit. 'I have asked around the area but no one else has reported seeing him at that point.' And then I decided I ought to mention the Arab and the Indian – from the tone of his conversation, I wondered if he already knew about them. And I added a note about the cavalier's dress too, expressing my belief that it might be the same man dressed in different outfits – the fact he was tall and fit, and always running, were, in my view, material aspects of his description.

'Well you did what you could, and what-ever the fellow dresses in, I cannot see he has committed any offence, well, not to our knowledge, that is,' he nodded. 'It's just one of those weird things that cross our paths from time to time. I agree it's wise not to refer to the cavalier in your accident report – just say it was a man, as you have done. It would only prompt silly questions from Divisional Headquarters.'

I was relieved to hear his reasoning and then, one chilly and rather misty morning in November, I was due to perform an early turn patrol, beginning at six and terminating at nine, following which I would have a break for breakfast.

Afterwards, I'd continue my duties until two in the afternoon. But it was that first three hours for which a route was laid down – I had to visit Elsinby, Maddleskirk and Crampton and so I left my house in the Mini-van, having allowed the engine to warm through before setting off. As a rule, these morning routes were devoid of people on the roads, save for the occasional early morning workers – people like bakers, chefs, newspaper delivery boys, window-cleaners, farmers, lorry drivers and postal workers might be encountered but not many members of the general public.

As I pottered around my route, checking vulnerable properties like the explosives store at Thackerston Quarry, a few empty houses and commercial properties and out-lying farm buildings, I found myself chugging along an unsurfaced road through the dense pine forest above Maddleskirk. It was an eerie experience because a thick mist enveloped most of the conifers; it was rather like driving through a long foggy tunnel and I startled a few deer, a fox and several owls and wood pigeons, but otherwise the drive was featureless – although I drove slowly and with great care due to the unsurfaced road and the all-enveloping fog. I continued along this route because it was a short cut through the forest and took me into Maddleskirk via the west end of the village, effectively reducing my trip from an isolated barn by three or four miles.

As I had some twenty minutes before making a rendezvous point outside Mad-dleskirk Post Office, I pulled on to a hard surface in the forest, switched off my lights and engine, and settled down for a five-minute break with a flask of hot coffee and a chocolate biscuit. The interior of the van was warm and I enjoyed my drink. Through the windscreen ahead of me, I could see the lane between the trees – the density of the conifers meant each side of the road was pitch black, but the road, with the canopy of fog above it and the brightening sky above that, extended like a line of light directly ahead. It was not daylight by any means but I could see some distance ahead. After a few minutes of silence and solitude, I became aware of a bobbing head; it was black and rounded and it was coming towards me. It was a running figure, I realized, a man judging by his general appearance.

I could see his head bobbing up and down against the lighter skyline and my first thought was that it looked like a motor cyclist running while wearing a crash helmet. As he approached, I sensed it might be the man reported earlier – the running Arab, the Indian and the cavalier – the clues were there. A wooded area, a running figure, a man who thought he was alone ... and now he was only yards ahead. In a trice, I flicked on the headlights and leapt out of the van.

I heard him cry out in alarm and, as he turned to dart away into the cover of the forest, I shouted. 'Police!' My shout echoed in the stillness of the morning as I heard myself repeat. 'Police. Halt!' Usually, that does the trick!

I wondered if my sudden and unexpected action would panic him further, but he halted in his tracks and I found myself looking at a city gent. He was a tall young man wearing a bowler hat, a black dress jacket, black and white striped trousers and carrying a black rolled umbrella. He was dressed like one of those London office workers of the period, and was panting heavily, either from fright or exertion.

'Good morning,' I greeted him.

He was now standing with his hands on his knees and his body bowed as he tried to regain his breath, and then he straightened up and said, 'You gave me a real fright ... I never saw you ... and putting those lights on like that...'

'Sorry,' I said. 'I saw you running towards me and decided I'd like a chat.'

'A chat? Out here at this time of morning?' He spoke with a cultivated accent. I now felt I had found my Arab, my Indian and my cavalier.

'I don't want to alarm you or detain you, but have you recently – well, earlier this year – dressed in other outfits? An Arab, say? American Indian? Cavalier?'

'There is nothing wrong in that, is there?' he frowned. He was in his early twenties, a tall, fit-looking man.

'A man dressed as a cavalier startled a driver recently...' I began.

'It was me, but I didn't run into the road, you know, I stayed on the verge. I think he must have been half asleep or something. Am I in trouble for that?'

'No,' I said. 'We're not pursuing that enquiry, not officially, that is. Now it's just idle curiosity on my part, no more than that. I've had reports, you see, during recent months, of a man running in the woods or down by the river, sometimes as an Arab, sometimes as an Indian and that time as a cavalier. And I believe the cavalier called the ambulance to the scene of that accident ... it's puzzling me, that's all. There is no criminal offence to bother me, no likelihood of an arrest, no publicity: just curiosity, I assure you.'

He smiled and straightened up, now looking rather more composed as he moved from the direct gaze of my headlights. 'And now you have a city gent in the woods? A long way from London?'

'I have, and it increases my curiosity about this gallery of odd characters.'

'I like running,' he said. 'It's my way of exercising. I did cross-country runs at school and love it, so that's what I am doing. Keeping myself fit by continuing my cross-country runs.'

'I can understand that,' I said, 'but why the fancy dress?'

'I don't want to be recognized,' he admitted.

'Really? Well, you are rather high profile in the clothes you've chosen as your running gear!'

'But not as high profile as my normal everyday clothes,' he countered.

'Which are?'

'I'm a novice monk at Maddleskirk Abbey,' he admitted. 'I didn't feel it right to run around in my habit, neither did I feel it right to wear shorts and singlets for these runs in public places – I have access to those – so I dress up in something fairly bizarre so that no one will recognize me.'

'What about a track suit?' I suggested.

'Wonderful idea, but I have no belongings, I am a monk. I have no clothes of my own, Constable. Maybe my mother will buy me one if I drop a strong enough hint. I think she thinks I can have everything I want from the community, but not many abbeys have a stock of track suits.'

'But they do have stocks of Indian outfits? And Arabian robes? And enough clothes to mock up a Laughing Cavalier?'

'We run a private school as I am sure you know, and we have a theatre and a wonderful stock of theatrical costumes in our wardrobe department, for our various school productions. I borrow those ... it seemed a good idea, and most of the time no one sees me ... and if they do, I know they do not recognize me. I think it is better to see an Indian running than a monk in his habit ... monks must always be aware of their public image.'

'Rather like policemen,' I said. 'I was once told I shouldn't ride a bright red racing cycle while dressed in my uniform, but it was all right to use a sit-up-and-beg type of ancient black bike. And I could not have ridden on a donkey at Whitby or Scarborough while in uniform, or do the tango with a beautiful woman...'

'Then you'll understand my dilemma?' he smiled.

'I do,' I said. 'Well, I'd better let you go. But you've solved a mystery for me and I shan't say a word to anyone.'

'Yes, I must get back before the school and

abbey lay staff begin to arrive.'

'I can give you a lift,' I offered. 'I'm heading for Maddleskirk.'

He looked at his watch (a permissible personal possession, I guessed) and said, 'Yes, I think I would welcome that.'

And so I returned him to his abbey and dropped him outside the theatre building. I never told anyone I had solved the mystery of the running men: I thought it best to leave things as they were, a rather endearing and harmless local mystery.

At Christmas, though, a regular at the Hopbind Inn, an Irishman called Seamus O'Hagan, told me he'd seen Father Christmas running through Elsinby Woods. I asked him if someone had spiked his beer and he merely chuckled and shook his head. 'No, it was real enough,' he assured me. 'I know Father Christmas when I see him!'

'You'll be seeing leprechauns next,' I joked.

'No I won't; you only see them in Ireland,' he told me in all seriousness.

In the 1960s and earlier, a certain mystique surrounded the powers of observation, and even the powers of deduction, possessed by police officers. Not all of us were like Sherlock Holmes but some members of the public thought we were.

Much of this highly acclaimed aura was erroneously caused by the detective stories and films of the era. Detectives, both those from the private sector and the police, were credited with almost super-human powers. For example, people thought a policeman could memorize every face that he saw during his tour of duty, or recall the registration numbers of all vehicles stolen in the district, or commit to memory every item for sale in a gift shop or on a market stall. There is little doubt some police officers did possess photographic memories – I knew one who could scan the football results which were published in the Saturday evening newspapers, and then recount them accurately over a pint or two later in the evening. Another could memorize all the words and obscure provisions of an Act of Parliament and then write them all down with amazing accuracy – he had no trouble passing his promotion exams, although it is doubtful whether he actually understood what he was reading or writing. There have been instances when police officers have recognized a wanted person in a crowd in the street having seen his photograph many months earlier, and in my own case, I arrested a man who had stolen a raincoat from a dance hall two years before – although I must admit it was my own raincoat! But I did recognize it!

It follows that if a policeman says he has seen something strange he will usually be believed – after all, the powers of observation possessed by most police officers are highly developed and such officers are superbly trained in the skills of accuracy in their accounts of what they see; their evidence must be beyond dispute. So, when PC Alf Ventress, the stalwart veteran constable of Ashfordly Police Station, reported the sighting of a UFO, few doubted his word. After all, lots of people from lots of places around the world were seeing flying saucers and other unidentified flying objects, so why not PC Alf Ventress?

I learned of this excitement one Thursday because I was enjoying a couple of weekly rest days at the time of the sighting. My days off were a Tuesday and Wednesday in late June, and it was on the Wednesday that Alf was patrolling my beat in the Ashfordly-section car. He was paying periodic visits to the villages on my patch during his own working day.

It was a somewhat dull day with persistent cloud, outbreaks of drizzle and even a threat of thunder but, from time to time, the sun broke through briefly to bathe the landscape in a bright glow before being lost again behind a towering lump of something like a strato-cumulus or cumulonimbus. Alf, with nothing to occupy him except to keep the car on the road for the period of his eight-hour tour of duty, was pottering along a narrow, little-used lane between Aidensfield and Crampton. The lane ran along the northern side of a ridge of land known as Crampton Rigg; the carriageway ran slightly below the summit of the ridge which meant that the view to the south was obstructed by that chunk of land. All that could be seen to the south was a series of rising fields, hedges and occasional copses. As one drove east along this lane, Crampton village and its church tower became very prominent while to the north lay the distant moors with a broad valley separating them from Crampton Rigg. As the lane had been created about halfway up the ridge, it provided a wonderful view across to the north, extending for several uninterrupted miles and taking in umpteen small villages and distant towns.

By knowing which direction to look, it was possible to identify Eltering, Brantsford and even the edge of Ashfordly along with villages like Slemmington, Lower Keld, Briggsby and Stovensby, while the slopes of the moors above Gelderslack were also visible on a clear day. Visitors to this part of Yorkshire would often halt along the lane to enjoy the panoramic view to the north. Regular callers, such as delivery vans of all kinds, vets, doctors, nurses, the milk lorry, the postman and others would also stop to savour the delights of this peaceful and panoramic stretch of landscape. I had often come across commercial travellers parked on the verges and enjoying a few minutes' relaxation – and I'd done exactly the same myself when having to while away a few minutes prior to an appointment.

Alf Ventress had been doing precisely that. He'd been due to make a rendezvous point to meet Sergeant Craddock outside the post office in Crampton at 3 p.m. that Wednesday afternoon. It was a routine meeting – the sergeant would be touring around in the course of his supervisory duties and this was one way of making sure Alf covered the required ground during his patrol. With some twenty minutes to pass away before his meeting, Alf had pulled on to the verge, taken out a cigarette and lit it while sitting in the driver's seat to admire the view. And, as he gazed into the distant blue yonder, he'd seen the UFO. At first, he'd not been sure what he was looking at and, knowing Alf fairly well, I knew he would screw up his eyes, gaze at the thing, probably throw his cigarette out of the window, cough and splutter and then try to determine precisely what he was seeing. He'd done all that, I am sure, for he then radioed Eltering Police Station. There was no one at Ashfordly Police Station because Alf was out here in the car, and so, by calling Eltering, he hoped to contact someone in authority. But by the time he'd established contact, the thing had disappeared: Alf prematurely terminated the call.

'Delta Two Four, are you trying to establish contact?' called the constable from Eltering.

'Two Four receiving,' acknowledged Alf, adding, 'Yes I was, but the situation has changed. Cancel the call.'

'Understood, Control Out,' said the anonymous voice without questioning Alf's decision.

Having seen the object, though, Alf had

been very shaken by the experience and it was some time before he could gather his wits, light another cigarette, and then be a few minutes late making his point with Sergeant Craddock.

'Problems, PC Ventress?' Craddock's eyebrows were raised as Alf parked outside Crampton post office and alighted from the car, now without a cigarette but looking somewhat shaken. 'Three o'clock means three o'clock, you know, not six minutes past!'

'Sorry, Sarge.' Alf looked pale and shaken. 'But I've had a bit of an experience.'

'Really?' and those eyebrows had been raised again.

'I've just seen a UFO, Sergeant,' muttered Alf, not being sure how his sergeant would react to the news. 'Just along the lane, a few minutes ago … then it vanished.'

'Really?' And Craddock's eyebrows had performed another of their hairy-caterpillar arched-back movements. 'And, pray tell me, what was it doing?'

'You don't sound as though you believe me, Sergeant.'

'Well, I wouldn't say that, but I have known constables to fall asleep in their cars and have dreams, and those cigarettes of yours are mighty powerful.'

'Sarge!'

'And then at lunch-time you might have sampled something stronger than tea or coffee…'

'I never drink and drive, Sergeant, and I have not been seeing things.'

'I thought you said you had been seeing things?' smiled Craddock. 'So just tell me what you saw, no embroidered account, just the facts, PC Ventress.'

'I was parked along that lane, the one that comes in from the Aidensfield direction, Sergeant. I stopped to pass away a few minutes before meeting you. I was looking north, out of the car window, and I saw an object in the sky. It was moving.'

'Ah! Go on. What sort of object?'

'Well, that's the trouble. It was cigar shaped with a wide middle and narrower ends, back and front. Like the side view of a saucer, well, two saucers together, face to face, if you understand. Fat in the middle and narrower at the edges. And it was silver, gleaming silver. It was moving fast in the sky with the sun glinting from it, fairly high … east to west direction over the moors. I watched it, Sergeant, and then it just vanished. It just seemed to vanish into thin air.'

'An aircraft, PC Ventress. A conventional aeroplane, I am sure. There is an old airfield in that valley, is there not?

'At Stovensby, yes, but they don't fly from there, not now, not since the war.'

'A large kite, then? A model aircraft? Do they fly model aircraft from that old airfield? Or balloons? A reflection on the clouds ... it could be anything, PC Ventress. How large would you say it was, this object?'

'Well, I don't know, Sergeant. I couldn't say how far away it was, but it seemed a long way off, too far to get a clear view in fact.'

'I don't quite know what to make of this,' Craddock said. 'I am not saying I doubt you, PC Ventress, you are a trained observer so perhaps you'd better make a report, for the record. Just be factual, don't elaborate and don't speculate. And don't tell the Press!'

'Aren't we supposed to report this sort of thing to the authorities, Sergeant? To the Air Ministry or whoever? There's been a lot of sightings in recent months; that saucer over the moors above Harrogate, and that sausage-shaped thing in the Lake District, the one with smoke coming from its tail-end, and then that carry-on in America where a woman said she'd been abducted

179

by aliens...'

'Yes, well, we have to be selective. I think you should make a detailed written report and I will forward it to Divisional Head-quarters so that a higher authority than you or I can decide on the right course of action.'

'Well, yes, I suppose so, but it was quite an experience, Sergeant, quite unsettling to be honest. I mean, it's not every day you see a flying saucer, is it?'

'Indeed not, PC Ventress, indeed not. Anything else to report?'

'No, nothing else, Sergeant. All quiet otherwise.'

'Good, then you proceed to Ashfordly Police Station to make your report. I am off to Eltering now. I will mention this to the inspector so he will be ready to decide on the right course of action.'

And so Alf had driven back to Ashfordly Police Station shakily to make his report and that is how I came to learn about his experience. In addition to making his written report for Divisional Headquarters, he placed an entry in the Occurrence Book, the daily diary which was maintained in every operational police station, and that is where I read it the following morning. Alf was manning the office at the time.

'All right, all right, Nick, I know you don't believe me, no one does, but I know what I saw.'

For what must have been the hundredth time, he recounted his experience and I listened intently. Clearly, Alf had seen something puzzling and quite alarming, but exactly what he had seen was something of a mystery. Unidentified flying objects on Aidensfield beat? Flying Saucers over the North York Moors? I decided that all I could do was to maintain observations! After all, the thing had been observed from a vantage point on my patch.

About a fortnight later, I was travelling along that same stretch of isolated road and the weather conditions were almost identical to those experienced by Alf Ventress. Like him, I parked on the verge, not to admire the view, but to check some documents before calling at Crampton Estate Office on an enquiry about one of their commercial vehicles. It had allegedly been sighted in Leeds without a road-fund licence and I was *en route* to see the estate manager. And as I packed away the papers in my brief-case, I saw the cigar-shaped object moving rapidly through the heavens.

From my vantage point, it was just below the horizon of the distant moors, moving swiftly and smoothly across the valley with the sun glinting from the silvery fuselage; exactly the scenario witnessed by Alf Ventress. It was just like two saucers together, one upside down on top of the other. The part not reflecting the sun was black – it did look cigar-shaped… Alf had not made up his tale, and I knew he had seen something inexplicable.

And then, as the object turned towards me and disintegrated, I realized it was a flock of racing pigeons out on a training flight.

Flying as one, speeding through the heavens, at a distance, with the sun glinting from their white feathers, they looked just like a flying saucer or cigar-shaped object, but as they turned towards me, the outline changed and I realized they were birds. In Alf's case, he had completely lost sight of them, probably due to the distance; but I had not.

So, should I report to Sergeant Craddock that I had seen a flock of racing pigeons being exercised on my patch? Or should I continue to let Alf and Craddock believe that flying saucers were operating on Aidensfield beat?

I decided I would keep my thoughts to myself. I wouldn't offer my explanation for Alf's sighting. After all, it was possible he had seen something else, a real unidentified flying object perhaps?

Chapter Seven

During market-days in the small towns dotted around the North York Moors, one of our duties was to patrol among the stalls with our eyes wide open, just in case some shifty dealer was attempting to use this means of disposing of stolen property. It was a simple and very effective means of distributing stolen goods, not only to gullible purchasers, but also to the wider public, including unsuspecting experts.

This was not a large-scale or major problem, however; any high quality antiques would rarely, if ever, be deliberately sold by market-traders, although it was possible that some small and rare object might find itself displayed and sold as a trinket. Oil paintings, rare books and items of jewellery might sometimes be sold from market-stalls, as would items of glassware, ceramics or what was loosely termed bric-a-brac and genuine bargains were sometimes discovered among what appeared to be miscellaneous pieces of utter junk. I recall a book dealer picking up a shoebox full of old books, swiftly checking its contents, paying a very low price for the boxful, and then rushing off with a look of total glee on his face. I was later to learn that among those old books he had spotted a rare and very valuable Bible and had bought it for next to nothing.

Most market-traders and antique dealers can tell similar stories, but deals of that kind were not of any professional concern to the police. What we sought was stolen property, but when faced with a large market-stall full of assorted oddments, probably having been transported over a long distance and collected during a lengthy period, it was virtually impossible to recognize anything which may have been stolen. To outward appearances, all the goods on view had been placed there for legitimate sale and it would be a mammoth task to check every item to see whether or not it had been reported stolen. Although most thieves disposed of their hauls very quickly, some did safely store them in the hope they would be forgotten, and after the passage of an appropriate time, would produce their treasures from a safe hiding place in the hope of a trouble-free sale or disposal.

When accepting a report of stolen property, the most difficult thing, from an operational police point of view, is obtaining an accurate description of stolen items. When I was in the Force, many people who lost valuables could not provide a detailed description of their belongings and, quite often, the description they produced was insufficient as any kind of legal proof of ownership. Whilst a man might recognize a statue of Venus stolen from his garden, how could he prove it is definitely his, especially if the seller also claimed ownership and if thousands of identical statues had been manufactured? A stolen object needs some means of positive identification if it is to be restored to its rightful owner; this might be a serial number, a crack in a certain place, a piece missing through damage caused by the true owner, some attempt to repair or colour it, some mark placed there by its owner ... almost anything, in fact, so long as it applied only to that item and within the knowledge of the true owner, thus making the most ordinary of objects unique. Things like bicycles, television sets, washing-machines and even cameras might bear serial numbers which provide proof of ownership, but most antiques did not carry such recognizable features.

Another difficulty in detecting crimes which involved stolen goods was the slow pace at which descriptions or even photographs were distributed among police forces. The police service did possess its own information system and whilst something like a car registration number or serial number of a stolen television set could be rapidly circulated by police radio, it took much longer to issue a photograph or drawing of, say, a stolen oil painting, longcase clock or piece of furniture. It could take days or even weeks for news of such a theft to be distributed nationwide. If a burglar got away with a really big haul, say from a museum or art gallery, the newspaper industry showed us how speedily it could provide images of the lost items, images that reached a huge audience among the public as well as the police, and this made me realize how the Press could aid the police in detecting crime. But making use of the Press as an aid to detection was a step too far in the 1960s! We had to stick to our traditional systems, even if they were dreadfully outdated.

In spite of our difficulties in tracing stolen goods, some of the traders believed that police officers possessed high powers of observation along with a knowledge of everything that had been illegitimately obtained and so we felt that, to some degree, our uniformed presence around the markets did deter some villainy. Perhaps we deterred only very localized villainy; perhaps local thieves did not attempt to dispose of stolen goods through the local markets, but in spite of our rather modest efforts, I am sure lots of stolen items were sold through market-stalls, probably without the stall-holder knowing their doubtful origins. And, of course, if a purchaser buys an object on the open market the *market overt* – and pays a fair price for it, – then he has a legitimate claim to that property, even if it is later found to be stolen. Such battles over ownership could often be settled only in a civil court, not through the criminal process of law.

It was with all these facts at the back of my mind, therefore, that I encountered Claude Jeremiah Greengrass one Friday morning as he stood behind a stall on Ashfordly Market. I had not noticed this stall on previous market-days and guessed it was yet another new Greengrass enterprise. He was selling what appeared to be a load of old stones. His battered and rusting lorry was parked behind his stall and when I peered into the rear, it was also full of large pieces of stone and other bits of what looked like smashed pieces of reddish pottery.

'So what's all this, Claude? A job lot of old stone?'

'Can't you read?' he grunted at me, and pointed to a handwritten sign which said, "Buy a piece of Roman rock for your garden – original stone from a Roman Villa".

'Roman rocks?' I smirked. 'Nobody's going to fall for that one, Claude!'

'They're genuine, Constable. If you look at some they've got dates and lettering on them … in Latin. Most of those have been sold but I've had to hang on to some to prove they came from the same places as those without letters and dates. I wouldn't be surprised if Julius Caesar had used some of these bits for his palace, or for a bit of dry-stone walling. And those brick coloured bits are pottery, vases or summat. All Roman.'

I picked up some of the pieces and examined them.

Some of the stones were small, about the size of a man's fist while others were considerably larger, several even extending to eighteen inches in length by some nine or ten inches in width. Most seemed to have been carefully shaped at some stage by a stonemason, although the smaller pieces appeared to have broken away from larger chunks, rather than being individually dressed. The pieces were all local limestone, a pale golden colour in keeping with the houses of Ryedale and when Claude directed my attention to those on his stall, I saw that some did appear to bear lettering or figures of some kind. Even if the lettering was faint and weather-worn, it seemed to be very ancient, so much so that I could not decipher any of the words. What he described as pottery appeared to be pieces of terracotta with dark grey on the outside, rather like slim portions of vases or urns and on one item I saw some letters very faintly incorporated in the piece. In my very ill-informed opinion, ENIA, looked like part of a word or name, and the broken edges told me the beginning and end of that word was missing.

'All right, Claude, next question: where did you get this stone? And these bits of pottery or whatever they are.'

'Now that's something I'm not going to reveal, Constable, I have a private supplier, quite legal and legitimate, and he wants me to act as his agent in selling it because he hasn't time. It's all good Roman stone, Constable, from a Roman villa which my contact happens to own.'

'He owns a Roman villa?'

'Aye, well, it's on his land so he must own it, mustn't he?'

'I'm not quite sure of that, Claude, I have no knowledge of archaeology or the rules governing the discovery of ancient buildings. All I know is that such finds don't come within the scope of the laws on treasure trove. They apply only to finds of gold or silver, or items containing gold or silver, not stone or pottery. Anyway, I'll buy a piece from you, and a bit of that terracotta with those letters on. If they are Roman, it might be nice to own a piece of history before it gets lost!'

And, in exchange for a few pence, I acquired a fist-sized chunk of greyish-tan limestone and a piece of the broken terracotta-like pottery bearing the letters ENIA. I bore these trophies home and placed them on the desk in my office, thinking I might use them as paperweights. A day later, Mary hailed me.

'Nick, those bits of stone and stuff on your

desk, are they important or can they be thrown out? It's not evidence of some kind, is it? Somebody been throwing stones in glass houses?'

I explained how I had acquired them and she said, 'Well, I hope you're not going to keep them for ever, they make dust and so far as I can see, they're just like any other bit of stone or broken pottery. I don't want to spend my time moving and dusting stones which would be better placed in a rockery.'

'I was hoping I might find out where Claude obtained them,' I explained. 'If they are from a Roman villa, they could be important, historically, I mean.'

'You asked where he'd got the stone?' she put to me.

'I did, but he's not saying. He reckons he's selling the pieces on behalf of a third party, but I'm not sure whether I believe that.'

'Well, if the stones are not stolen, there's not a lot you can do, is there?'

'No,' I had to agree.

Mary accepted their presence on my desk, if a little grudgingly, as I decided I would endeavour to trace their origins. The area around Aidensfield was rich in Roman history; York was a key location in that history, but Malton, known to the Romans

192

as Derventio, was another major centre of Roman activity. Leading west from Malton was a Roman road which even today has generated the suffix 'le street' after the names of some villages like Appleton-le-Street and Barton-le-Street. That ancient route stretched across the countryside and crossed the summit of what is now called Ampleforth Beacon to lead up the ridge of a hill towards Sutton Bank Top. Even now, the section of the road which crosses the moors above Ampleforth is known as High Street – even though it is a long way from Ample-forth's main street. Delivery vehicles find the name confusing because there are only two remote farms along High Street! But the road is high in the hills and follows the route of the earlier Roman street.

Amongst the network of Roman roads which once dominated this area, one remains to this day. It is nicknamed Wade's Causeway and it runs across Wheeldale Moor near Goathland. Much of the stone from the original Roman road has been plundered for the construction of farms, houses and other buildings, and in times past a good deal was removed to form the foundation of modern highways, such as the route from Stape to Egton Bridge. Some stones were almost removed to build walls around the intakes of land on the moor.

In spite of all this vandalism, however, a remarkable section of the original Roman road still exists. Dating from AD 80 and 600 feet above sea level, it is about a mile and a quarter in length and comprises a sixteen-foot wide road made of flat stones on a bed of gravel. Raised in the centre to facilitate drainage, there are side gutters and culverts – it is a structure way ahead of its time when we consider the state of our English roads, even until the time our railways were being created. Wade's Causeway is said to be the finest surviving example of a Roman road in Britain. Beyond its southern tip are the puzzling Cawthorn Camps, believed to be a Roman signalling station, while beyond its northern end, the route heads for the North Sea via Grosmont and Briggswath, probably terminating at either Whitby or Golds-borough. It is called Wade's Causeway because our forefathers, knowing nothing of its origins, thought it had been built by a local giant called Wade.

Close to this route, and around Derventio (Malton) there were many Roman villas. They were places of industry which included quarrying, metalworking, farming, livestock breeding, pottery-making, and at Norton, near Malton, there was even a goldsmith's shop managed by a slave. The villas were impressive buildings with heated rooms, baths, tessellated floors, painted walls, granaries and even horse- or donkey-mills. These wonderful places were luxurious by any of the prevailing local standards, but the local peasants would probably have only worked there. Evidence of their existence was all around Aidensfield – at Lastingham, Gillamoor, Castle Howard, Beadlam, Baxtons near Helmsley, Hovingham, Helmsley itself and Hood Grange near the foot of Sutton Bank.

In 1612, a Roman sarcophagus was found at East Ness near Nunnington and it bore the inscription. 'Valerius Vindicianus had (this tomb) made for his wife, Titia Pinta, aged thirty-eight, and his sons Valerius Adintor aged twenty, and Varoilus aged fifteen'. Ness is known for its spring waters and one might speculate that these young men died protecting that water source from invaders.

It was against this background of Roman settlements that I wondered if Claude's supplier had unwittingly discovered one of those villas or perhaps a portion of a former

Roman road. Such discoveries did occur from time to time and in the past, if a landowner found a deposit of beautifully cut stones buried on his land he would simply make good use of the materials. Well-cut stone was always in demand for drystone walls or repairs to buildings. There was no thought of preserving the site or informing interested parties or authorities, especially if they were likely to disrupt the vital yearly cycle of farming by excavating the area.

For some weeks afterwards, Claude and his pile of stones made irregular appearances at Ashfordly market and I learned that he had also attended markets in Eltering, Brantsford and elsewhere, always with his pile of 'Roman' stones. Although I, and others, tried to elicit from him the source of his supply, he steadfastly declined to reveal it, and he managed to sell a substantial number of pieces. People liked the idea of a Roman rockery, for example, or a garden footpath made from stones upon which Julius Caesar may have trod during his visit to England, or a wall made from stones which might have been part of a Roman bathroom.

And I still had my piece of stone which served well as a paperweight.

The mystery behind Claude's enterprise receded to the back of my mind as the weeks progressed, and as we'd had no reports of ancient sites being plundered, or other sites being newly discovered, my desire to trace the source of the stones began to evaporate. And then, as so often happens, a welcome coincidence occurred when I had a small duty to execute at a farm well off my own beat. The village constable of Slemmington, PC Jim Collins, was enjoying a couple of weeks' annual leave and, as his section, Brantsford, was now operating in conjunction with ours (Ashfordly) under Sergeant Craddock's supervision, and the constables of Ashfordly Section took turns to patrol his beat. My turn came when we received a message from York City Police to say that a Mrs Nancy Scott of Coldharbour Farm, Slemmington, had witnessed an accident in Lord Mayor's Walk, York, and that Mrs Scott should be interviewed and a witness statement obtained from her. A car had collided with a cyclist and Mrs Scott had both witnessed the incident and given first aid to the injured bike rider.

One dull and mild Wednesday afternoon in June, therefore, I drove to Coldharbour

Farm having first telephoned to ensure Mrs Scott would be available. This was not the hill country to which I was accustomed, but a lush and low-lying area of Yorkshire. I found my way through the leafy lanes, negotiated a level crossing, passed over a hump-back bridge and after travelling for almost a mile beside a slow-moving stream, saw the impressive entrance to Coldharbour Farm.

This was not a hill farm where a farmer suffered a tough existence, but a well-managed, spacious and prosperous-looking arable farm specializing in cereals and root crops of various kinds. I drove along a tarmac-surfaced road and into the clean and open yard. I parked beside a Landrover and went to the door, there to find a note saying, 'Just popped down to the buildings'.

There were buildings all around so I began my search, touring lots of barns and open-fronted stores before I heard voices and the sounds of activity coming from what appeared to be a new barn. I ventured inside. Several workmen were busy; clearly, this was a new structure and it was still in the process of being built although the walls and roof were in position. I had no idea which was Farmer Scott, but as there was only one woman there, with a trayful of mugs of tea, I guessed she was Mrs Scott. Dark-haired, attractive and in her early fifties, she wore a pair of light tan slacks, a T-shirt and sandals.

'Ah, PC Rhea, I was expecting you,' she smiled a genuine welcome. 'You'd better come to the house. You're just in time for a mug of tea.'

She led me back to the house via a short cut through the complex, and it was then I spotted the pile of stones on some rough ground among nettles and briars, behind the new building. Even from a casual glance, they looked remarkably like those Claude had been selling on his market-stall, but I decided not to mention them at this point. I would first complete the purpose of my visit.

Over a mug of tea and some home-made buns, I obtained her witness statement – she had a clear memory of the accident and I knew her evidence would enable York Police to decide whether or not to prosecute the vehicle driver concerned.

Then I said, 'As we came here, I couldn't help noticing that pile of stones behind the new building...'

'Oh, those!' she sighed. 'When we decided

to build the new place, our contractors wanted to check the ground to see if it was satisfactory for the foundations and they came across all those stones. They ummed and ahhed as to whether to leave them and bury them under concrete, or alternatively unearth them and make completely new foundations – which is what they decided to do.'

'So what are they?' I asked.

'Well, we don't really know. Ted, that's my husband, thinks they used to be a building of some kind. They're all neatly cut and trimmed … this is a very ancient farm, Mr Rhea, no one is quite sure how long there's been a settlement here, and we wondered if there'd been a cottage under our new barn in medieval times, or perhaps some other farm building … the contractor laughed and said it looked like a bit of a Roman road to him, but I think he was joking. He said we should remove them and maybe use them for walls or something, so we just unearthed them all with the diggers – some bits of pottery came up too – and made new foundations for our barn.'

'Has Claude Jeremiah Greengrass been in touch with you about them?' I asked.

She smiled. 'Yes; when the contractor first

hinted they might be Roman, Claude happened to be here, he was taking away some of our old farm machinery to sell. He got his eyes on those stones, asked if he would sell some, on a shared profit basis with Ted, and so Ted agreed. Claude loaded some of them into his truck and off he went, saying he'd sell them as tourist souvenirs. Why are you asking? Have we done something wrong?'

'Not that I'm aware of,' I tried to reassure her. 'But I think those stones could be genuine Roman relics, some of the pottery has an inscription on it, and one or two of the stones Claude sold also had an inscription on; it looked like Latin to me.'

'Oh dear, you don't think we've ruined a Roman road or something, do you? We did have discussions with the planning people and so on, while we were deciding what to do and where to erect that new barn, and nobody said anything about reporting any discovery of buried stones. We decided to put the building there because we've tried to plough that area in the past and found it too stony; the whole of that field is very stony, Mr Rhea, not just the bit where we've erected the new barn.'

For a few moments, I did not know how to

approach the possibility that this could be a significant discovery, if indeed it was Roman remains, and I guessed the Scotts would not want their farming disrupted by archaeologists and other experts working on their premises for what might be a long period. I felt I should place the onus on the Scotts and so, after a moment's thought, I asked, 'Mrs Scott, just suppose your farm was sitting on top of a Roman road, or even a Roman villa?'

'Yes?'

'What would your reaction be?'

'Well, I don't know, Mr Rhea. Ted and me have never been ones for historical stuff and we know nothing about such things. I wouldn't know a Roman stone if I saw one and neither would Ted, although years ago a chap told us this farm might be on the route of a Roman road, or even the site of a villa. He said all farms called Coldharbour used to be along Roman roads, but I've never heard that before ... but those stones were under just one small corner of the new barn. If there's more, they'll be outside the limits of the new building, under land we've not been able to plough because of the stones. I can't see Ted objecting if the experts came along for a look, not out there; it's not in our way. We've been unable to make use of that piece of our land and there's a separate lane leading to it, it comes in through the back of our premises.'

'I bought some stones from Claude,' I said. 'If you don't mind, I could show them to a contact of mine, he's an archaeologist in York, and get his advice.'

'I'd better have words with Ted first,' she said. 'Shall I ring you when I've discussed it with him? I can do it tonight, over our evening meal rather than disturb him just now.'

And so that is what I arranged. Later that same evening, Ted Scott rang me and expressed great interest in the notion he might be living on top of a Roman site of some kind, or very close to such a site. He said his contractor had told him to get rid of that pile of stones – I could understand why, especially when I discovered that the contractor in question did a lot of work in York.

In that ancient city, almost any excavation reveals an historic site of some kind. Some contractors don't want their work to be interrupted and many were tempted to keep such discoveries secret. Ted, however, felt that if his farm had any such historic links, they should be made known and agreed that

I should first approach my contact; meanwhile, he'd not allow Claude to remove any more stones. To cut short a long story, my York contact, Adrian Medway, looked at my two trophies and immediately rushed to Coldharbour Farm to inspect Ted's pile of stones as well as several bits of terracotta and said, beyond doubt, they were Roman relics. He said it was almost certain that Coldharbour Farm occupied the site of a Roman villa which had stood beside the Roman road which ran from Amotherby near Malton to join Wade's Causeway at Cawthorn, and so continue across the moors towards Whitby.

Much later, when Ted and Nancy gave their approval for the archaeologists to excavate the rocky piece of ground behind their new barn, they discovered the wonderfully preserved site of a former Roman villa; only a small corner was missing – and that had, for the most part, been sold by Claude Jeremiah Greengrass. These stones I'd seen in a pile at Coldharbour Farm were gathered to make a feature in a local folk museum and – much to Mary's delight – I donated my two pieces to that cause. Although it had been impossible to determine the wording on the few stones which bore inscriptions,

Adrian believed that the portion of a word on the terracotta was the name of the potter.

It seemed that pottery made by a man called Genialis had been found in other parts of the area, with similar discoveries around the Humber and as far away as Norfolk and Leicestershire; on some pieces, his name appeared as Genia.

For many months and even years afterwards, the patch of land behind Ted's barn was covered by a large green tent and although the discovery was regarded as very important, it was never open to the public during my time as the constable of Aidensfield. Later, I think Ted permitted a limited flow of interested people to inspect the villa in his back yard, but it was never turned into a public tourist attraction.

But I did wonder whether Genialis had ever sold his pottery in the local markets.

Claude's brief enterprise was not the only occasion when stones were sold in Ashfordly market. Up to a point, one can understand people wanting to own a piece of Roman history, but as I pottered around the market one Friday, off duty as it happened, I spotted a small group of objects at one end of a stall which was selling handicrafts of various kinds. When I looked closer, they were highly coloured solid shapes and painted upon them were names. Almost immediately, I spotted Pedro the Paperweight, Daniel the Doorstop, Freddy the Fish Tank (to place in the bottom of the tank), and Carlos the Car, the latter for placing under the tyres of cars to prevent them rolling away down hills.

There were others, but as I examined them, the stall-holder, a small middle-aged man with a big woolly jumper, materialized and said, 'You'd like to buy a stone?'

'Is that all they are?' I asked. 'I thought they might be glass or metal or a ceramic of some kind. They look nicely done.'

'They are nice works of art,' he grinned. 'But they are stones, polished and painted of course, then given a personality.'

'So who buys stones?'

'People who like them,' he beamed. 'Lots of people in fact. You might say to yourself that you would like a paperweight for your office and you could easily pop into a stationers' shop to buy one, or you could even use a stone from the garden, but here, Pedro is special. He's unique, a real asset to any office…'

'Do you paint them?'

'No,' he shook his head. 'No, they're the work of Glenys Page, she's a farmer's wife who lives in Gelderslack. She's too busy to stand here all day, so I sell them for her, on commission. There's the bed of an old stream behind her farm and she gets the stones from there, moorland granite for the most part, and she colours them. They're all smooth and nice to handle, and they come in various sizes and colours. There's little ones – pebbles – she does one called Millicent the Marble and another Clarence the Clay; then there's medium ones like those stones you're looking at, and larger ones she calls boulders. I don't have a boulder here today, but Benjamin the Boulder is quite a character, wonderful for anchoring your dog lead in the garden, or you could even use him for weight training. And Rudolph the Rock must be seen to be believed. You could use him as the corner-stone for a house or for weighing down the back of your car when there's snow on the road.'

All the uses to which he referred could be achieved without having stones painted with faces or other characteristics, but I quite liked the idea of a paperweight and so, for the princely sum of ten shillings, I bought Pedro.

'What on earth is that?' asked Mary, when I produced Pedro from my pocket when I got home.

'That's Pedro the Paperweight,' I beamed. 'I bought him for the office.'

'But it's just a piece of stone. You've only just got rid of Claude's Roman bits and now you've brought another ... Nick, you are the limit!'

'Ah, yes, but this one doesn't make dust, he's nice and smooth with a happy face and he'll stop my papers blowing all over the place when anyone comes into the office. I can get you Daniel, if you wish; he's a doorstop.'

'Nick, we've got better things to do with our money than go around buying lumps of stone of the kind you can pick up free from the ground.'

'Ah, yes, but these are works of art, specially painted and unique. Pedro will be worth a fortune in the future, you'll see. It's the painting that is worth the money, not the piece of stone.'

I got a distinct feeling Mary was not impressed, but I was quite proud of Pedro. He performed a useful function in my office, sitting silent and still on top of my piles of official paperwork.

A few weeks later I had to visit Rockside Farm, Gelderslack, to check a firearm certificate. It had been issued to Richard Page, the husband of Glenys, and so I was able to call at the farm and see, in person, the lady who painted personal stones. A buxom lady in her mid-thirties, with a mass of bubbly blonde hair and a delightful smile, she produced a coffee and some biscuits for me. After I had dealt with the firearm certificate renewal, I mentioned the painted stones.

'It all started as a family joke,' she smiled. 'Richard was grumbling about his papers always blowing about his office whenever anyone opened the door – he likes to work with his windows open you see – so I said he should plonk a stone on top. He said the idea of a chunk of stone sitting on top of his important forms and letters was not very attractive, so I went down to the beck, found a nice round pebble, quite a large one, and painted a face on it. I called it Pedro and he loved it. Then a friend came in and said she wanted a doorstop – and it just went on from there. In no time, people were asking me to make personal stones for them and I decided I'd try and sell them.'

'Well, I have a Pedro I bought at the market,' I told her. 'And he's doing a good job. But there must be a limit as to what anyone can do with a pebble or a stone, even if it is painted!'

'You don't have to put them to work!' she laughed, with the infectious smile on her face. 'They are quite happy just sitting on the floor, or window ledge, or desk, or wherever. But I do have a speciality.'

'Go on, tell me,' I challenged.

Instead of explaining, she went into an adjoining room – her studio – and returned with a handful of painted pebbles. The largest was easily held in the palm of her hand. They were of differing sizes, I noted, each with some kind of numeral painted on top, and when she placed them on the table before me, I saw that each sat firmly in a small hollow on top of the one below. I counted eight in all, the largest at the bottom with all the others sitting on top in a tier.

'This is the Waite family,' she smiled. 'Spelt Waite but really weight.'

'They're weights?'

'Yes, for a set of kitchen scales. I found them by chance. The biggest is exactly one pound, the next is eight ounces, then four ounces, two ounces, one ounce, half an ounce and the little one is just one quarter of an ounce and that very tiny one on top is an eighth of an ounce. I've checked their weights; they are accurate. And you'll see the weight of each is painted on them. There you are, PC Rhea, a set of weights, unusual and only available from here.'

Fascinated, I picked up the stones and held them in my hand, all rounded and comfortable to hold, then recalled that Mary had once complained that the set of ancient kitchen scales she'd inherited from her grandmother could not be used because she could not find a complete set of weights. They were available, she felt sure, in specialist shops or even on antique stalls, but she'd never been able to find a complete set. Modern scales did not use those old fashioned brass weights. But here was a complete set, right before my eyes. Not in brass, admittedly, but a complete set of kitchen weights which were suitable for the scales she possessed.

'Do you have just the one set?' I asked, thinking it must be very difficult finding stones of the exact size, weight and shape. That little depression in the top of each would be a deciding factor, and then the weight had to be precise... I thought the whole idea was amazing.

'I've four complete sets and several incomplete ones.' She dazzled me again with that smile. 'The hard part is finding the right stones; it means scouring the old river-bed time and time again, but the right stones are there, all I have to do is find them. I've discovered that there are certain places they seem to assemble, where the flood waters of the past have washed them and where the action of the water over the centuries has formed them into these shapes and sizes. They are there, Mr Rhea, in my secret quarry! It means, of course, that these sets are rather more expensive than the paperweights and door stops. But they are unique, I don't think you'll ever find any of these sets anywhere else.'

'I'm surprised you want to sell them,' I put to her.

'Well, at first, I did not think I'd find any more stones, but when I did, I made a second set of weights, called them the Waite family, and sold them. I have the original in my studio – not for sale under any circumstances, I might add.'

'So how much do you want for these?' I still had the stones in my hand, weighing them up and down in my open palm as I felt the smoothness of the heavy stones.

'Twelve pounds,' she said. 'I know it's a lot for a handful of stones...'

'I'll take them,' I said on impulse.

Mary thought I was more than just plain mad, paying almost a week's wages for a pile of stones from a moorland river-bed but when I demonstrated that they were accurate and that they did the work of a conventional set of kitchen scale weights, she mellowed and in time, grew to like her unique set of weights. A few months later, she discovered a complete set of brass weights on a market-stall, exactly the sort to match her inherited scales, so she bought them for use in the kitchen. The Waite family was allowed to recline in safety on a high shelf to avoid damage and to maintain their shiny features. It was a few years later when an artistically minded friend popped in, saw them and offered Mary £25 for the set. I was pleased to hear her say, 'Oh, no, I can't sell these, they're unique. I wouldn't part with the Waites for all the money in the world!'

And she never has.

One curious fact related to market-stalls

was made evident one Friday as I patrolled the busy square in Ashfordly. It was around lunchtime and the first influx of market shoppers – locals and tourists alike – had come and gone. Before the second rush of more locals and tourists during the afternoon, there was usually a lull around lunchtime. It was during this temporary break, especially in the holiday season, that the more discerning of local people went to Ashfordly to do their banking and shopping. Because the early local shoppers and tourists had moved on to other places and the afternoon rush had not yet materialized, there was a brief oasis of calm which allowed the residents the brief chance of finding a parking space.

Finding a parking space not occupied by a tourist in the holiday season was tantamount to finding a little patch of heaven, especially for the elderly who needed a car conveniently close to the shops and banks. It was during one of those lulls, therefore, that I was patrolling Ashfordly town and I wandered through the market, now much less busy than an hour earlier. The stallholders were making the most of the temporary period of tranquillity and some had left their stalls for a quick pint of beer and a sandwich, with a neighbour keeping an eye on their wares, while others were lunching behind their counters.

As I strolled past the huge fruit and vegetable stall, with two attendants enjoying their fish-and-chips from newspaper, I noticed a small patch at one end of the stall. It had been cleared of the fruit and vegetables on sale, and instead it bore lots of full brown paper bags all neatly twisted at the top. I did not count them but there would be about two dozen, all roughly the same size and large enough to contain something like a pound of tomatoes or grapes, or some mushrooms. I had no idea of their purpose or what they contained, but one of the stall-holders, a small, happy man I knew only as Charlie, noticed my interest and called out with a wide grin, 'Presents from our customers. That's what they are.'

'Presents?' I stopped and must have had a puzzled expression on my face.

'Aye,' he chuckled. 'Not given willingly, I might add, but we regard them as presents. Summat that helps us make a decent profit.'

'I don't follow,' I had to admit.

'They're full of fruit or vegetables,' he explained. 'Stuff bought by customers and then forgotten about and left on the stall.

You'd be amazed how many folks, women especially, buy stuff, put it down while they find their money, then walk off without it. Most of 'em never miss it till they get home, and then it's too far, or too late, to come back for it. Tourists especially, they buy stuff and leave it when they go off to Scarborough or Whitby and never come back. We put it all to one side, like you can see, so if they do return looking for their stuff, it's all there waiting for collection. You can see we've had a good morning already! The afternoon's yet to come.'

'I can understand one person leaving stuff occasionally, but I'd never have guessed it would be such a regular occurrence,' I laughed.

'You'd be surprised how much stuff we collect in a week, and what isn't picked up before we close down is returned to stock, we've no alternative. It'll sell somewhere next day, well, most of it will. Here, I'll show what we've got so far!'

He picked up one of the bags and opened it. 'See, a pound of nice fresh tomatoes...' Then another, 'Grapes,' and another, 'Broad beans...' And then, 'Hello, this 'uns something mighty heavy. Potatoes, I'd say.'

But when he opened it, he almost dropped

the bag and his face went ashen as he said, 'It's a hand grenade, Constable. God, what do I do with this...?'

'A hand grenade?' I wondered if he was playing some kind of joke on me and went for a closer look. Sure enough, it was a hand grenade and I could see no sign of any pin, the extraction of which would detonate the thing.

'Put it back very gently,' I said. 'On the ground, out of reach, where no one's likely to pick it up or kick it...'

'Is it alive?' He was shaking now. 'I mean, will it go off?'

'The pin isn't there,' I said. 'That means it could have failed to explode when the pin was withdrawn which in turn means it is still dangerous. Just put it down, Charlie, very very carefully ... whatever you do, don't put it in a bucket of water, keep it dry, and then get as far away as you can... I'll report it now; I'll get the bomb disposal people to come and have a look at it.'

'But if it goes off, all my vegetables and fruit will be blown sky high.'

'And so will you if you don't put it down very very carefully. Now, I'll have to evacuate the market without causing panic ... but first, put it down.'

I waited, trying to be as calm as I could, as Charlie placed the grenade very very gently into a box of oranges and then he rushed off. 'Charlie, don't panic, keep calm...'

'I'm off,' he said. 'There's no way you'll catch me standing near that thing. Come on, everybody, move, out of here...'

I had to take control.

'Attention please!' I shouted in my loudest voice. 'Everyone. Could everyone please move away from the market-square, get behind one of the buildings. We've found a hand grenade, it looks old, but it could be dangerous. Please do not panic. Just walk away, leave your stalls, leave your shopping, and get clear.'

It was mighty hard work, making everyone listen and then persuading them that this was a serious matter, but with a lot of help from the stall-holders, we eventually cleared the market. I then radioed Sergeant Craddock.

'Sergeant,' I said in as firm a voice as I could muster, as I stood with a good view of the market, trying to prevent newcomers from entering. 'I have just evacuated Ashfordly market. An unexploded hand grenade, with the pin missing, has been found on one of the stalls. Can we get the bomb disposal people here please, as soon as possible? The device is now under the fruit stall, in a box of oranges. The entire market has been evacuated.'

'Are you sure it's a real one? It's not a model, is it? Or a toy?'

'Sergeant, I have no idea. It looks like the real thing to me. It's heavy enough to be the real thing and the firing pin is missing. To me, that spells danger.'

'All right, PC Rhea, you maintain a discreet distance and protect the public, I will ring the bomb disposal unit.'

It took an hour for the experts to arrive during which time I, along with Sergeant Craddock, PCs Ventress and Bellamy, had immense difficulty persuading oncoming people not to venture into the market, now deserted by people but still bearing the image of a busy place due to the stalls. I indicated the whereabouts of the offending object and the team of two soldiers went about their task with all the calmness one had come to expect. They located the grenade, examined it and pronounced it live. It dated from the Second World War, but for some reason it had not exploded when the firing pin had been extracted. That meant it could still be dangerous. With their traditional skill and care, they bore it out of the market and into the grounds of the castle, the nearest patch of open land. Once it was out of the market, the stall-holders and public began to drift back – but every stall was examined in case any more grenades were lurking in abandoned paper bags or elsewhere. Shortly afterwards there was a modest explosion somewhere behind the ruined castle and a few sods of turf were thrown into the air.

'All clear,' the bomb disposal officer told me when he returned. 'It was live, I reckon you know that now, but we've detonated it. So where did it come from?'

That question was never answered. No one came forward to admit leaving the grenade among the fruit and vegetables, so we had no idea who had left it there or why they had left it there, but afterwards Charlie and his pals always made sure they knew what was left on their stall, carefully check-ing any brown paper bags before placing them aside for collection.

Chapter Eight

It was mid-morning as I was executing a foot patrol which included the market-square of Ashfordly. Along one of the narrow sidestreets, just outside the Fire Station, was a telephone kiosk and at 10.45 a.m. I had to stand beside it for five minutes in case Ashfordly Police Office, in the shape of the sergeant or PC Alf Ventress, wanted to contact me. In those days, of course, patrolling constables did not have personal radio sets and so it was the practice, every hour during our patrols – or in some cases every half-hour – to stand near a designated telephone kiosk for five minutes so that the office could contact us if necessary. As a consequence, we knew the location of every telephone kiosk within miles.

And so it was that I stood outside this particular kiosk to await any messages from the office – a report of a stolen car perhaps, or a request to attend some incident in the town, or just an update on the current state of a known travelling villain or some other police matter. There were no messages on this occasion, but just as I was about to leave, a smart red Morris Mini eased to a halt close by. It contained four people, two young women and two young men, and they looked rather like Polynesians or Singaporeans, or perhaps someone from another race whose facial characteristics were similar to those of the Chinese. I was insufficiently experienced in my knowledge of foreigners to recognize their race. The front seat passenger, a man, climbed out and approached me. He was carrying a map and looked rather nervous.

I smiled and said, 'Good morning.'

He returned my smile and bowed ever so slightly, then said in a very strong accent, 'Good morning and excuse me.'

'Can I help?' I did not want to frighten him for I knew that some foreigners had reason to be afraid of police officers.

The map and his demeanour suggested he was lost and in need of directions, then he opened the map, pointed to Ashfordly and uttered something I did not understand. I pointed to Ashfordly, prodded the map and nodded furiously as if to say, 'Yes, you are here.'

'Ah!' His face lit up. 'Ah, here!'

'Yes, here,' I continued to nod furiously. 'Ashfordly.'

'Ah! Ashfordly,' he said. 'Ah, here!'

Meanwhile one of the girls had lowered her window and called across to me in a form of English I could hardly understand, but I caught the words, 'We wish to visit the monkeys.'

'Ah!' It was now my turn to say. 'Ah. The monkeys?'

The driver nodded and the girl nodded, and now that I understood, I indicated I could help them. A new zoo, based in the hall and grounds of a nearby country estate had recently opened. It was flourishing in the midst of the North Riding of Yorkshire and within a matter of months had become extremely popular – and I happened to know it contained a wide variety of monkeys, apes and chimpanzees. The country house was Weston Hall, the area around it being known as Weston Park with the new zoo named as Weston Park Zoo and Gardens.

Its extensive acres boasted a natural lake, a wonderful garden, woodlands, open fields and lots of hothouses and enclosures for a variety of animals, reptiles and insects. There was a picnic area too, along with a shop and a cafeteria. I guessed these over-seas visitors would enjoy it. I took the map, laid it on the roof of their car and indicated the zoo. By now both the driver and the girl were standing beside me looking at the map, nodding furiously as my finger stabbed the place which I said was 'Monkeys' and then traced the route from Ashfordly town centre through Brantsford and Eltering, and along the country lanes to Weston Park. They followed my finger with nods and chatter as I highlighted Brantsford and Eltering, and the turn-off leading to Weston Park. Once they approached the zoo, it would be well signed and I felt they would have little difficulty locating it.

'Monkeys?' the girl smiled, stabbing the area marked Weston Hall.

'Yes, monkeys,' I nodded vigorously, and confirmed it once again by stabbing the map and finger-tracing the route from Ashfordly. After much more nodding and smiling, they returned to the Mini, waved at me, turned around and departed. I watched them drive slowly through the town, turn right at the junction and disappear on their trip to visit the monkeys, a journey of around twenty-two miles from where I stood. I hoped they would have a nice day and felt pleased with my action – after all, part of our training was to be helpful and courteous to everyone, especially visitors from overseas. I completed that tour of duty at 1pm and went home for my meal break, and in the afternoon I had to patrol the area around Aidensfield, including Maddleskirk, because the Maddleskirk village constable was away on a course.

I was scheduled to finish my day at 5pm, one of those rare occasions when a constable works the sort of hours enjoyed by others. At 4pm I had to make a rendezvous point – my last of the day – outside the telephone kiosk beside the post office at Maddleskirk Abbey and so I made for the abbey in my Mini van. I parked and climbed out to potter around the exterior of this huge, busy abbey – not a ruin but a living monastery – and then I saw the same little red car I'd seen earlier in Ashfordly. It was coming towards me containing the same four earnest young people and, as it stopped, I waved and smiled at the occupants.

'Ah!' said the driver, as he climbed out and recognized me.

'Ah!' I smiled. 'You had a good day, seeing the monkeys?'

'Ah, here monkeys,' and he pointed to the

main entrance to the abbey.

I shook my head. 'No, monks here, monkeys in the zoo.'

'Monks?' His brow creased in thought. 'Monks here?'

I nodded. 'Monks here,' and I pointed to the main entrance and then, as luck came to our rescue, a monk appeared and headed for the post office.

'Monkeys here!' he beamed.

'Monk,' I said.

Or had he said 'Monk is here?'

But it was clear that he was now at his intended destination and laughed as he explained the error to his friends who saw the humour of the misunderstanding. I then watched them drive into the main entrance of Maddleskirk Abbey to visit the monks – not the monkeys.

I have no idea what kind of day they had at Weston Park Zoo looking for monks but it seemed to have kept them cheerfully occupied until now.

This short tale provides a good example of the occasional difficulties we experience in trying to understand one another. In this case, it reminds me of a story told to me by a monk – he taught religious studies at the village Catholic school in Maddleskirk and was teaching the children to say the Hail Mary. The opening words of that famous Catholic prayer (the Ave Maria) are: Hail Mary, full of grace, blessed art thou amongst women...' But when he asked the children to write down the words, one of them put '...blessed art thou, a monk swimming'.

This is like the child who inherited a battered old teddy bear with cross eyes and called him Gladly because he'd heard someone quoting 'Gladly, my cross-eyed bear' (Gladly, my cross I'd bear). And there was the woman who thought the Countess of Ayr was coming to lunch when in fact it was the county surveyor. Another gem is the story of the father who tried to explain to his young son the tale of Lot and his wife. The father told the child, 'God said to Lot – "Take your wife and flee from the city, but do not look back". But Lot's wife did look back and was turned into a pillar of salt.'

'So what happened to the flea?' asked the fascinated child. You've got to read the story out loud to appreciate the child's question.

As a policeman in a busy tourist area, I was often asked for directions from be-wildered visitors. The one thing that frequently surprised me was the number of motorists who embark upon a long-distance journey without a map. They depart from home with a vague notion of driving towards their intended destination, but then rely on other people to direct them. If the person giving the directions does not fully understand the question, or if the pronunciation of place names is wrong or misheard, then chaos can result. Drivers can finish miles away from their intended destination. When I was a serving policeman in Whitby, on the north-east coast of Yorkshire, I was regularly called upon to calm the nerves of tourists who thought they were in Whitley Bay, which is almost seventy miles further north on the coast of Northumberland. I recall one taxi driver who was asked to collect a passenger from York Station and convey him to Clapham. The passenger went to sleep in the back seat with orders to be roused upon arrival, and he was highly surprised to be awoken in Clapham, South London when in fact he wanted Clapham, a small village in the Yorkshire Dales near Skipton. And Londonderry on the A1, a few miles from Bedale in North Yorkshire is often mistaken for its namesake in Northern Ireland – while Bedale is pronounced locally as Beadle. Confusion occurs also when several villages have the same name – there are umpteen Thorntons in North Yorkshire and more than just one of the following: Aislaby, Appleton, Brompton, Burton, Carlton, Danby, Easby, Hutton, Marton and Nawton. Norton near Malton in Yorkshire is often confused with Norton near Stockton-on-Tees in Cleveland, and Nawton near Helmsley can add to the confusion. Constable Burton in the Yorkshire Dales gets mixed up with Burton Constable in the East Riding and the pronunciation of Harome confuses most.

The county has some wonderful village names the likes of Sexhow, Fryup, Kettlesing, Foxholes, Horsehouse, Glasshouse, Silpho, Potto, Stank and Booze. One Yorkshire village glories in the name of Yockenthwaite but is pronounced as Yokennut; another spelt Ruswarp is pronounced Russup; Wass is Woss; while Rievaulx is Reevo (even if some locals call it Rivis) and Jervaulx is either Jervo of Yervo. Both Rievaulx and Jervaulx are the names of ruined abbeys.

If the British people have difficulty understanding one another, then one can appreciate the problems facing visitors from overseas. I am often surprised how well they cope with our regional accents and dialects because these very localized modes of speech can even confuse the British people – a man chattering in the broad Geordie dialect, or one of those brogues from the depths of the Yorkshire Dales may find himself completely misunderstood, or not understood at all, by a Cockney taxi driver or a Norfolk villager.

We had such a problem in Ashfordly when Sergeant Craddock, whose Welsh accent seemed out of place on the North York Moors, received an emergency telephone call. It was a cold and damp Tuesday morning in February and I was pleased to be working in the tiny police office which adjoined my house, catching up with some report writing. As a general rule, village constables spent the first hour of their shift working in their own office attached to the house; this enabled them to deal with correspondence and reports and it was advertised on their notice-boards as a time when the general public could contact them about routine matters.

That particular morning, therefore, I was finishing some admin. work before driving into Ashfordly to present several files to

Sergeant Craddock. But shortly after nine, he rang me, and sounded agitated or excited.

'PC Rhea' – his voice sounded sharp and almost curt on the telephone – 'I need you in my office immediately, a matter of importance and urgency.'

'Yes, Sergeant, what is it?' I asked, wondering if I had to prepare anything before leaving. Was one of my reports overdue, for example? Had I omitted some important information from that recent crime report about the thefts of tomatoes from greenhouses on an Elsinby allotment?

'I will explain when you arrive, but it involves translation of a telephone call. We need to act with the utmost speed.'

'I'm on my way,' I assured him.

When I arrived, the duty office was deserted and so I went towards his office, tapped on his door and he called, 'Enter.

'Ah, PC Rhea.' There was almost a sigh of relief in his voice. 'Glad you could get here so quickly. Sit down.'

I did so and awaited his next move. 'A matter of translation, you said, Sergeant.'

'Indeed, yes. Seconds before I ran you, PC Rhea, I received a telephone call and I think it is from a local person, a male voice. No name, though. The caller did not give his name or address. That is the trouble: I do not know who the caller is and I cannot ask Ventress because it is his weekly rest day today and he's gone fishing.'

'So what was the call about, Sergeant?'

'I think he was telling me there is a body in the river, but I do not know where to begin to look and I cannot ring the caller because I don't know who it was. To be honest, PC Rhea, I hardly understood a word he said. But I did jot down something...'

'Right, fire away, I'll see if it means anything to me.'

'The man said something like this. "It's Jack Ron Ooze, thool hettigit devour foss doonby aye beaver, there's a body in t'watter". And then he rang off.'

'Did he say anything else?' I asked. 'No phone number or name or anything?'

'No, that's all I heard. Now as you know, I am not very *au fait* with your North York Moors dialect and I'm sure I have not written it down correctly, but that's how I heard it, PC Rhea. Apart from that bit about a body in the water, I haven't the faintest idea what he is talking about. But if there is a body in the water, we must get there as quickly as we can.'

'If it is a body, there's no great urgency, Sergeant; if it was somebody alive who was drowning, then the farmer will have got there to do whatever he can, a long time ahead of us. He does say it's a body.'

'I appreciate that, but can you translate it for me? I know you spoke the dialect as a child in these moors but that call doesn't make any sense to me.'

'If I had heard the message myself, Sergeant, I would have understood him, but getting it second hand, in writing, from a Welsh speaking person – well, I must admit it does not make a lot of sense. Can you give me a few minutes to decipher it?'

'If there is a body, we need to get there quickly, PC Rhea; time is of the essence.'

'Yes, I know, Sergeant, but it's no good rushing out like headless chickens before we have any idea where we're going.'

'Well, it's obviously somewhere near water, but I'll give you a few minutes' peace and quiet in my office. I will be in the duty office and will deal with any callers or phone calls. So, head down, PC Rhea, get your translating cap on! Quickly as you can, mind you!'

And so he left me alone with his scrap of

paper. I read it again. *Jack Ron Ooze, thool hettigit devour foss doonby aye beaver, there's a body in t'watter.* The end of the call, about there being a body in the water, was quite clear and I was sure that was exactly what the caller had meant. Reference to *foss* was also indicative of a river because foss is a local name for a waterfall. This made me think the location was somewhere on the banks of the local stream or gill, not a larger river meandering slowly along the floor of one of the nearby dales, but a fast-flowing moorland beck with a waterfall. I left the desk and moved to the map on the wall, of Craddock's office. The River Rye flowed down from the moors and along the floor of the dale towards Malton, and, as it neared Malton, the moors receded further and further into the background. To the west of Ashfordly, however, were the southern hills of the moors, precipitous in places with becks or gills dashing from the heights and at this time of year (February) they would be full of rushing water, the result of melting snows and heavy rain. There would be fosses galore on the moors!

Tracing the route of one with my finger, I was looking for some clue about the foss to which the caller had referred, realizing there

234

could only be a waterfall if the beck tumbled from a considerable height. In some cases, the word 'force' was used instead of foss, indicating the power of water flowing over a cliff or down a steep hillside. However, not every foss was large enough to justify its name on a one-inch map – and then I realized what the caller had meant by 'devour foss'. That was the Welshman Craddock's way of writing down his words – but I wondered if the caller had said, 'tiv oor'. That would mean 'to our' – add the word 'foss'. Thus I got 'to our foss'. This now meant the preceding words became easier – *hettigit* split into two gave me *hetti git. Git* means 'get' in our dialect and *hetti*, or *etti* means 'have to'. Thoo is a local word for 'you' – and so *thool* was really 'thoo'll'. Now I had a sensible sentence. In our dialect it would read, 'Thoo'll etti git tiv oor fos...' or 'You'll have to get to our foss'. I then realized that *doonby* in Craddock's note was 'down by'. So far, so good. A meaning-ful phrase – You'll have to get to our foss down by...'

And now I was stuck. Where on earth, or what on earth was *aye beaver*? And who or what was 'Jack Ron Ooze?' I decided to ask Craddock to repeat the latter in the hope I might catch some inflection in his voice which would aid me.

'Sergeant;' I returned to the duty office and his eyes brightened.

'Success?' he asked.

'A little,' I said. 'But can you repeat Jack Ron Ooze as near as possible to the way the caller used it?'

He closed his eyes in an effort to revive his memory and said, 'Yak Ron Ouse ... yes, it sounded something like that.'

'Yak? Not Jack?'

'Well, yes, I suppose it was yak. I thought it was his name, you see, Jack Ron something or other ... jack and yak can sound very similar in certain conditions, and, well, Ron is a man's name.'

'And ouze?' I put to him. 'Did the word ooze sound as it does in oozing, or ouse, like the River Ouse?'

'Shorter than both,' he nodded. 'Almost like *us,* but a fraction longer.'

'Oose?' I put to him. 'Could it have been oose?'

'Yes, oose. That's it, you sound just like him. Oose.'

'Right,' I said. 'That's the address. Yackron Oose, or ouse.'

'What on earth does that mean?' he asked.

'Yackron is the dialect for acorn,' I told him. 'And "oose" or "ouse" is the way of saying house. So the address is Acorn House. A lot of farmers answer the phone by giving their address rather than a name, and they do likewise when making a telephone call. So this call has come from Acorn House, Sergeant, wherever that is. Judging by the map, I think it must be somewhere in the Shelvinby area; there are several moorland becks which tumble from the moors in that area. I'll check the map again. If we can find an Acorn House – which will surely be a farm – we can get on the road and work out what *aye beaver* means as we drive there. At least if we get to the farm, we'll be told where to find this body.'

Together we scanned the map along several moorland becks which rose on the moors above Shelvinby and tumbled from the heights, over rocks and down cliffs, as they made for the gentler River Rye in the dale below. And then Craddock found Acorn House. It was on the eastern banks of Blaeberry Beck.

In the police office, we had copies of the electoral registers for all the villages and market towns which lay within our section

237

and it was the work of a moment to ascertain that Acorn House was occupied by a family called Stone – Richard and Helen were shown as the householders. A further check with the telephone directory showed that R Stone of Acorn House, Shelvingby was also listed there.

'Let's ring, just to be sure,' said Craddock, who then said, 'You'd better talk to him, PC Rhea, he might not understand me! Just confirm we are on our way.'

When I rang, a woman answered and I asked, 'Mrs Stone?'

'Aye,' she acknowledged.

'It's Ashfordly Police,' I told her. 'Your husband rang earlier?'

'Aye, 'e did.'

'Just to confirm we are on our way,' I said.

'He's down there now,' she said, and after a pause, added, 'waiting.'

'There's a body, he told us.' I needed to know if an ambulance was required.

'Aye,' she confirmed. 'A body, dead.'

'We'll be there very shortly,' I confirmed. This was sufficient confirmation for Sergeant Craddock to head up the dale to Acorn House and we arrived within fifteen minutes or so.

I was the driver and eased the car into the

farm yard at which Mrs Stone, a sturdy lady in her mid-fifties, emerged to greet us.

'Thoo took thi time,' she muttered. 'Oor Dick's been doon there ages, waiting.'

'So where is he, exactly?' I asked.

'Whey doon 'igh beaver,' she said. 'That's what he told that sergeant chap when he rang. That it was doon bi 'igh beaver.'

As she spoke the words, I realized that *aye* in Craddock's notes should have been 'high'. High Beaver. So what on earth was High Beaver?

'So how do I get to High Beaver?' I asked her.

'Straight doon yon field.' And she pointed to a track. 'He's gitten 'is tractor, thoo'll see it, parked in 'igh Beaver.'

'So what is High Beaver?' I asked. 'Another farm? A cottage?'

'Nay, lad, thoo knaws nowt! It's yan of oor fields. 'Igh Beaver's above Low Beaver and that's next ti Little Buttercups on yan side and Tall Trees on t'other ... all fields, they are, all doon there. 'E's waiting, and 'e's been waiting quite a bit...'

So we set off and Sergeant Craddock laughed. 'So the message I got really meant: this is someone calling from Acorn House. You'll have to get to our waterfall down by that field we call High Beaver because there's a body in the water.'

'That's about it, Sergeant; we're nearly there.'

Dick Stone was as stout and uncommunicative as his wife and we found him standing by his tractor. I drew our car to a halt at his side and we climbed out.

A black and white collie dog was sitting on the seat and Dick, in his early sixties I guessed, was smoking a large briar pipe.

'Thoo gat 'ere, then,' he said, turning, and without another word, headed down the slope at a very fast pace. The dog leapt off the tractor and trotted at his side, occasionally looking at us and doubtless pondering our purpose. We had almost to trot to maintain his pace, but, as we hurried down the slope, I could hear the sound of a waterfall among the beckside trees below us, and across to my left, could see the glistening of the water as it rushed and tumbled from the moors.

'What sort of a body is it?' I panted, as Craddock and I struggled to keep pace with the farmer.

'It's a deead 'un, Constable, a chap; rambler by t'leeak of 'im. 'E's been deead a lang while, Ah'd say.'

To cut short a long story, Farmer Dick Stone led us down to the beckside and along a narrow footpath which followed the line of the banks. Quarter of a mile downstream we came to the waterfall, a roaring mass of white water which crashed over a ledge some ten feet high and dropped into a deep, peaty-coloured pool before flowing over rocks and boulders on its way to join the main river. Dick led us down the path which descended between the rocks beside the waterfall and after a further hundred yards or so downstream, he pointed to what looked like a pile of wet clothing.

'That's 'im,' he said, and halted, as Craddock and I went forward to inspect his discovery. It was the sad remains of a white-haired man whose body was dressed in hiking gear and walking boots.

Judging by his appearance, he had lain in this deserted spot for a long time because much of his flesh had been eaten away by the effects of the weather, or the activities of wild animals, birds or even insects. He was wearing a waterproof jerkin and I fished around in his damp pockets in the hope of finding some kind of identification, eventually discovering a water-logged wallet. I opened it to find a name among the contents – Henry James Preston, with an address in Birmingham.

'Radio Headquarters from the car,' Craddock told me. 'See if we've any record of him; he might have been reported missing.'

Leaving the carcass, we trudged back up the hill with Farmer Stone leading the way, and, as we reached the waiting vehicles, Stone said, 'Well, Ah'll be getting on.'

'I'll need a statement from you,' I told him.

'Ah shan't be far away,' he said, without halting, and in moments he had vanished over the horizon with his dog.

Through the Force control room, we learned that Henry James Preston had been missing since before last Christmas. A bachelor, he had left home to go on a walking tour but his sister, with whom he lived, had no idea where he'd gone, except it was somewhere in the north of England. He'd assured her he would telephone every other day to report his whereabouts, but she admitted that when he said 'Heading for Brantsford this evening,' or something similar, she really had no idea where he was, or where his location might be found. When he'd failed to return home at the expected time – the middle of January – she had reported his absence to Birmingham City Police.

Without any evidence of him being the victim of crime, or suspected of committing crime, they had no authority to mount a search, although they had entered his name in various lists in case he was questioned about anything, or found wandering. His name was also recorded in the 'Missing from Home' files but these efforts were fairly low key and consequently no specific search had been mounted. Even if there had been a search, who would have thought of searching the waterfall below High Beaver in remotest Shelvingby? Later, when the body had been recovered and a postmortem conducted, the pathologist could find no reason for thinking his death had been suspicious – as Mr Preston was sixty-eight years old, it seemed he had died from natural causes, probably a heart attack. A later inquest returned an open verdict.

But at the time, I had my file to complete and that meant obtaining a statement from Richard Stone. After we had removed the body to the mortuary and asked Birmingham Police to inform Mr Preston's sister, I drove Sergeant Craddock back to Ashfordly, then returned to Acorn House to complete my paperwork. Fortified with mountains of scones and slabs of fruit cake and a mug of tea, I settled down with Mr Stone in his sitting-room to record his discovery of the remains.

It was a simple story – he'd been checking his sheep and had gone along the riverbank to see if any of his flock had strayed into the woodlands beside the water, and he'd then found the body. He'd never seen the man before; he'd not called at the farm for food or accommodation and Mr Stone had no idea who he was or where he'd come from.

Because the place he was found was not on a public footpath, it was something of a mystery as to why Mr Preston had followed that route. Dick Stone thought he might have got lost in one of the dense moorland fogs which sometimes smother those moors, especially in winter time, and he thought that the rambler had found himself compelled to take the obvious route to safety by following a stream on its downward course in the belief it would lead to civilization or even just a mere shelter.

I recorded all this in writing and finally, out of curiosity, I asked, 'Mr Stone, you call that field High Beaver. Do you know if beavers ever lived here?'

'Nay, lad, it's nowt to do wi' beavers. It sounds like beaver, ah know, but we've not 'ad beavers living wild in England since t' twelfth century, even if Beverley is named after 'em. Ah know we call this field beaver but it's name leeaks like Belvoir, spelt B.E.L.V.O.I.R. It means good view. Ah thought thoo'd have known that! There's neear wonder it tyook thoo sike a lang time ti git here.'

Another case of slight confusion arose when the president of Aidensfield Womens' Institute, Mrs Gloria Hepworth, rang to say she would like to discuss a small matter with me. I suggested she visited me in my office at ten the following Thursday morning to talk things over and she arrived on time. Mary produced a cup of coffee for us, along with some chocolate biscuits, and we adjourned into my tiny office. Mrs Hepworth was a very attractive woman in her forties, well dressed and confident with beautiful features, an admirable figure and blonde hair.

'My members want to raise funds for charity,' she began. 'We have discussed the matter at our meetings and we've supported different charities over the years. One of our members is a keen worker for the NSPCC and so we thought we would like to arrange a collection for them. Our members want to spend a day in Ashfordly, preferably on market-day when the town is busy, collecting money in boxes. We thought if several of our members helped, they could take it in turns and work in shifts, say two hours at a time, and stand at strategic places around the market and in other parts of the town. I don't want a house-to-house collection; what we want is a street collection.'

'It seems a good idea,' I agreed. 'So how can I help?'

'I thought there were some rules and regulations about this kind of thing,' she went on. 'Someone said I needed police permission.'

'It's not exactly police permission,' I explained. 'In this area, the Ashfordly District Council wants to know who is arranging collections in their streets, so your first job is to contact them. They keep a list of applications and the purpose is to make sure that two different organizations aren't collecting on the same day or in the same place. They don't want fights or disputes. Once you've got their go-ahead for your desired date, you'd have to visit Ashfordly Police Station and ask for a street collection permit. Sergeant Craddock, or whoever is on duty, will write it out for you. That specifies the date and place of your collection. Once you've got that, you can go ahead.'

'And there are rules about how we go about it?'

'Yes, but they're not very complicated. You must have closed boxes or tins for the donations, and every collector needs written authority from you, just in case they are challenged. They mustn't cause annoyance or obstruction to passers-by; no one must be paid for their services, and when it's all over, there has to be a set of proper accounts detailing the money collected and any expenses incurred. A copy of those accounts must be sent to the police authority. Most organizations who arrange this kind of thing give the donors a little flag or badge to confirm the donation. It's all simple as that.'

'Well, thanks, I thought it was much more complicated. So the first thing I have to do is ring the council to see if they approve my proposed date?'

'Yes – so what is your date?'

'We were aiming for Friday, the second of

August or possibly Friday the ninth. It's the holiday season and the town is always busy, especially as it's market-day.'

'If you want either of those dates,' I advised her, 'you'll have to act quickly. Obviously, the most popular dates are soon snapped up by other organizations and charities, and the council won't let two groups collect in town at the same time. If I were you I'd ring immediately.'

'Oh, dear, I'm going away later today, for a fortnight, and I've all sorts to finish before I leave…'

'Look, ring the council right now, from here. I'll get the number for you. Just mention your dates, get them reserved for you, then you can get the permit from Ashfordly Police Station later.'

'Thanks, that's good of you.'

So I picked up my receiver and dialled the number of Ashfordly Rural District Council offices.

The switchboard operator answered.

'I'd like the person who deals with street collections please,' I said, and at that point, I handed the phone to Mrs Hepworth. Sitting fairly close to her, I could hear both ends of the conversation.

Mrs Hepworth asked, 'Do you deal with

street collections?'

'We do,' said the man. 'A complaint, is it?'

'Oh, no,' she responded. 'Not at all. No, I want to arrange a street collection in Ashfordly and would like to discus it with you, select a date and so on.'

'Well, we do it every Tuesday in town, and get round the villages on the other days, love. So you want us to do a special in your street, is that it? Having a party are you? Or some big occasion?'

'Oh, no, there's no party. I want to do it myself, with helpers, make the collection I mean. Right around the town, on market-day.'

'Well, on market-day we can do with all the help we can get; you should see some of the stuff that gets left behind. But I can't see why you want to help us out. Is it some kind of school project or consumer research? You're not one of those time-and-motion people, are you? I don't think our union would want you checking on the way we do our job, missus.'

Before I could interrupt, she said, 'Oh no, it's not that. We'll be doing it for the NSPCC.'

'They haven't offices here, love, you must have got the wrong town. Have you tried

York or Middlesbrough? Unless it's a charity garden fête is it, out of town? Will there be a marquee? On private land? And how many do you expect to turn up?'

'Oh, it's nothing as big as that, no marquee or anything, although we might have a market-stall. And we don't want to go to York or Middlesborough, they're much too far away for us. And it's not a garden fête either. No, it's just an ordinary collection and we want it in Ashfordly on a Friday. So would August the ninth be clear?'

'An ordinary collection? August the ninth? I don't know about that. Hang on a minute,' and there was a lull. I now realized these two people were talking about two completely different things, but in seconds the fellow returned and said, 'August the ninth, a Friday. That's when we're in Elsinby and Stovingsby, but we do come to the market-place in Ashfordly after the market's closed and see to things there. On overtime mostly, when the stalls have all gone.'

'Er, can I interrupt?' I waved at Mrs Hepworth. 'I think the gentleman is misunderstanding your request.'

'Is he?' she frowned.

'I'm sure he's talking about dustbin collections...' and I gestured for her to hand

me the telephone. She did so, with puzzle-
ment all over her face.

'Hello,' I said. 'I think we're talking about
different things...'

'Who's that? I was talking to a lady just
now; where's she gone? So who are you?
Have you been listening in? Put me back to
her. I think she wants us to do a special for
her, for the NSPCC ... garden fête or
something.'

'No, I don't think she does. She wants to
talk about street collections.'

'We are talking about street collections.'

'She's talking about standing on street
corners with charity collecting boxes, not
emptying dustbins.'

'Is she? Then why's she ringing me? I'm in
charge of street collections, mister, dustbins
and waste-bins. And most certainly I'm not
a charity, although on my wages I sometimes wonder.'

'She wants the department that deals with
charity collections; she wants to see about
getting a permit to hold a collection for the
NSPCC.'

'Well, if she'd said that in the first place, I
could have put her through to the right
department. Where is she now?'

'She's here. So, can you transfer us?'

'Hang on,' he said.

And so Mrs Hepworth's call was transferred to the Clerk's Department where she spoke to a lady who administered the street collection she required. She got permission for August the ninth and later I heard she'd received some very generous donations. But I often wonder how far that conversation would have gone, or what the result might have been, if it had proceeded to an uninterrupted conclusion.

Chapter Nine

A large percentage of work undertaken by the police and other emergency services is as a result of members of the great British public being either stupid, careless or utterly irresponsible. The daft behaviour of some adults; both at home and beyond the domestic boundaries, is saddening to behold – all one has to do is to look around or read the newspapers to get a flavour of this surprisingly prevalent lowside of English public life. Football hooliganism is a glaring example, and wanton street violence is another, but smaller incidents include people getting lost while out walking and not informing friends or relations of their intended destination; being swept out to sea in rubber dinghies; driving the wrong way down the motorway; locking themselves out of the house; doing botched DIY jobs; lighting fires on tinder-dry moors or in forests; locking dogs and children in cars during hot weather; leaving the oven on while on holiday; dumping litter of all shapes and sizes; running out of petrol or failing to top up their car radiators. The list of silly and thoughtless acts is never-ending and the people who have to deal with the result of these idiocies are usually the police, the ambulance service, the fire brigade or the coastguards – and it is all at public expense. Recently, a man decided to light a cigarette while filling a jerry can with petrol at a service station – there was a surprisingly modest explosion and he was blown fifteen feet into the air, then landed, backside first, in an ants' nest. Apart from superficial damage to the petrol pumps and a few minor burns to his body, he suffered many bites from ants in his pants and required hospital treatment for that – and he was considered a very lucky person.

But why would an adult male be daft enough to light a match while pouring petrol?

From time to time, however, the innocent and even helpful actions of individuals can combine to create unexpected dilemmas. We had a wonderful example in Aidensfield one summer.

If you walk down Hawthorn Lane which leads to the isolated Thornton Farm to the south of Aidensfield, you will see a stone-built garage, large enough to accommodate a single car. It stands about halfway between the village and the farm, and is to the right of the carriageway on a wide grass verge. It has been there for years and looks somewhat incongruous because there is no other building nearby, not even a barn or shed of any kind. The farm lies deep in a hollow beside the river half a mile or so beyond, but the entire area surrounding the garage comprises nothing but open fields. A drystone wall runs behind the garage and forms the boundary of the lane. How the original owner of this isolated garage got permission to place it there is something of a mystery, but probably there was an agricultural structure of some kind on this site long before matters like planning applications were invented.

I became aware of the garage during my routine quarterly visits to the farm to check the stock registers and although I wondered why it was standing in such an isolated location, there was never any occasion to question who owned it or what it contained. Most of the times I drove past – only some four times a year – the sturdy timber doors were closed and the only indication of occupancy was bottles of oil or car cleaner on the interior window ledges.

Three tiny windows overlooked the lane; they were more like small oblong holes than windows, but in the past, buildings on the moors were built to keep out the weather, not to let in daylight or sunshine. A cat might have struggled through one of these windows had it been open, but they were too small to admit anything larger.

On one occasion when I passed, however, the double doors were standing wide open and in the wet grass in front of them I noticed the wheel marks of a car. I was driving at the time and did not stop to peer into the garage although, as I passed by, I noticed, at the far end, an old sofa standing against the wall, a pair of old cane chairs of the kind one might find in a conservatory, and some lengths of timber, the sort one might use to construct a rustic arch in the garden. There were other bits and pieces against the walls, but the garage was otherwise empty and there was no one in attendance. From that single observation, I knew the garage was currently in use.

It was some time later, during a visit to Malcolm Kelly who owned Thornton Farm, that I discovered the garage belonged to him, and that it was used by his mother,

Agnes Kelly, who was a widow. Malcolm was in his mid-forties and had taken over the farm on the death of his father, Jack. Agnes, a fit and energetic lady in her sixties, had bought a cottage in Aidensfield but, as it did not have a garage and she owned a car, she made use of that sturdy garage down the lane on the way to her son's farm, even if it was a considerable distance from her home. But, as Malcolm said, his mother didn't use her car a great deal. I think the building had originally been a kind of shelter for agricultural machinery, a tractor or some other piece of machinery being stored here for immediate use in the nearby fields.

Late one summer night at the end of August, a Thursday, with a strong breeze blowing, Malcolm had been working in his fields to the east of that lane and was returning home via that route. It was about half past ten and dark. He was on the tractor and as he approached the garage, he noticed the left-hand door was standing wide open. He thought the primitive wooden sneck had not operated properly and that the stiff wind had caused the door to blow wide open. He knew that his mother's car was not in the garage that night – it had been taken into

Bernie Scripps's garage for some work on the brakes and exhaust – but he thought the door ought to be closed. He had done this trick many times before – he eased his noisy tractor to a halt very close to the open door, reached out from the cab and gave the door a hefty push. It swung easily on well-oiled hinges and crashed shut. As it did so, the long wooden sneck on the outside dropped into place, effectively securing it. There was no key to the door, no Yale lock or anything of that kind – thieves did not operate in such places – but the huge wooden sneck was highly effective and it fell home with a clunk. Malcolm could see that the strong doors were now firmly closed and secure and they wouldn't blow open in the wind. Happy that he had done a useful job, he went home. At the time, of course, I knew nothing about this minor incident.

At half past eight next morning, Friday, there was a loud knocking on my front door and I opened it to find Mrs Gillian Heddon on my doorstep. She was crying and looked extremely worried and distraught, so I invited her in, taking her into my lounge rather than my somewhat austere office. She looked as if she needed some kind of help so I settled her on the settee and asked Mary to bring a cup of tea.

The wives of rural policemen were accustomed to such sudden arrivals and requests – it was all part of their unpaid service to the constabulary, and thus to the general public. Gillian, having settled on my settee with a cup of hot sweet tea, sniffed away her tears and then said, 'I'm so sorry, Mr Rhea, turning up like this, and in this state but I didn't know what to do or where to go…'

'Well, you're here now, so what can I do?'

She sniffed again and wiped her nose and eyes, then said, 'It's Geoff, my husband. He didn't come home last night … I don't know where he is or what's happened.'

She was a plain woman in her mid-fifties, a homely sort of person who had always prepared her husband's meals on time, and did his washing and ironing while raising a family of three nice children. She'd never had a job other than looking after the home, while Geoff had worked hard to maintain his house and family. He worked at a factory near Brantsford producing plastic household articles like dishes and washing-up bowls, parts for cars, aeroplanes and ships, and lots of other things including pieces for television sets and radios.

When I quizzed her about his disappearance, she said he always went out for a drink at the pub on Thursday evenings, and had recently taken to going for a brisk walk around the village before coming home. He usually returned about eleven, made himself a cup of warm milk, and went to bed. Quite often Gillian would be asleep when he returned – as she had been last night. She'd woken this morning to find he wasn't at her side. His daytime clothes were not in the bedroom; she could see he hadn't shaved or had any breakfast, and gradually, as she had puzzled over his absence, she realized he had not come home. The car was in the drive too, and all his office things were in their regular place; his brief-case was in the hall as usual. She had rung the pub and was told he had been in last night, quite early, but had left about nine o'clock to go home. He'd not been ill – but he'd not been seen since that time.

She had walked along the route he would have taken from the pub, but there was no sign of him lying injured or collapsed in the street. I established that he had no history of heart trouble or other condition which might cause a sudden illness and then, while Mrs Heddon was with me, I rang the surgery in Aidensfield and all the local hospitals to see if Mr Heddon had been admitted as a casualty. None had any report of his admission. I then rang my own Divisional Headquarters to see if anyone called Geoffrey Heddon of Aidensfield had been arrested or been involved in anything that might require his detention. Even if he was suffering from loss of memory, he might be carrying a driving licence or something bearing his name. But there was no record of him in any of our files.

I asked about his work, whether he was under any undue pressure or stress, but she shook her head, saying he was very happy at work and had just been promoted and there were no financial problems at home which might cause him to act out of character. He'd never done anything like this before, she assured me.

I wondered, as all police officers do on these occasions, whether another woman was involved somewhere in the background, but it is not an easy matter to plant such an idea into the mind of a very upset and loyal wife. I felt that if Mrs Heddon did suspect that he might be seeing another woman, then she must raise the issue and draw my attention to it. I did not wish to upset her further by suggesting something that might not be the truth.

I obtained a very detailed physical description of Geoffrey and assured Mrs Heddon that I would circulate this immediately to all local police stations and to those further afield. I asked her to supply me with a photograph as soon as possible. I had to consider the notion that Geoffrey could have caught a taxi from the pub last night and then caught a bus or train to start a new life. I had no idea why he might wish to do that – from what Mrs Heddon told me, he seemed to have a very content and happy personal life in a comfortable home, but I then had to remind Gillian that unless it was feared that her husband had come to some harm or was at risk, or that he might be the victim of crime or be suspected of crime, we could not mount a full-scale search for him. I had to inform her that, however dreadful it is for the remaining spouse, an adult may leave home and vanish; that alone is not a matter for the police. We could not undertake to search for everyone who left home of their own free will, although there were agencies who might help, like the Salvation Army. She assured me, very tearfully, that Geoffrey was not like that. He would never go anywhere without telling her and so, if he had disappeared, then it was almost certain he had come to some harm.

I assured her I would do my best to trace him, and suggested she returned home, to be available near the telephone in case Geoffrey called, and to ask around all her acquaintances and relatives. I promised I would revisit her later today, and in the meantime I would record Geoffrey Heddon as 'Missing from Home'. At least, if he was involved in some incident, his name would appear in our files. I watched her leave the police house, a very unhappy, shocked and bewildered person.

My immediate task was to ring Ashfordly Police Station with details of Geoffrey's disappearance and although Sergeant Craddock reminded me that we could not mount a search of the district unless we had evidence of the likelihood of harm befalling Geoffrey, he would record him as 'Missing from Home'.

During my patrols that day, I would make enquiries in and around Aidensfield to try and find some solution, even if, strictly speaking, it was none of my business, I knew that Gillian Heddon, and the villagers, would expect it of me. But even as I was preparing to leave my office to begin that day's patrolling, there was an unexpected development.

The bell of my office door rang and I opened it to find a tall, smartly dressed man standing there; in his late thirties with dark hair, glasses and a very erect stance, he looked very much a successful business executive. My immediate reaction was that he was a businessman looking for a particular address in my locality.

'Paul Naylor, Constable.' His voice sounded almost upper class and he held out his hand for me to shake, which I did. 'May I come in?'

I admitted him to the office and settled him on a chair beside my desk then asked, 'Well, Mr Naylor, how can I help?'

'My wife has not come home.' He came straight to the point. 'Not for the first time, I must admit, but most times I know where she is and what she's up to, but not on this occasion.'

'You mean she's seeing other men?'

'Good God no! She's not like that! What I mean is that she gets herself involved in things, Constable, amateur dramatics, poetry societies, discussion groups, good causes and whatever, and sometimes she has to stay away overnight. Her poetry group have weekend events, for example, and they'll stay in a nice hotel in the countryside to discuss their art. That sort of thing.'

'A busy lady.'

'And a good thing too! She needs something to occupy her. We've no children and I'm away a lot, I'm a rep for the building trade. I cover the north of England, from the Trent up to the Scottish border and that means I spend far too long in ghastly hotel rooms. But whenever Jean's going to be away, she always lets me know, leaves a note or phones me if I'm away, always. But this morning, when I woke up, there was no sign of her. No note, nothing, I got home late last night, you see, saw she wasn't around and, naturally, I assumed she was attending one of her things. I was shattered after driving all over Northumberland yesterday and crashed out in bed, then this morning – no Jean. No note. Nothing. But her things are at home – make-up, toothbrush, spare clothes, suitcase and so on. And her car. All there, Constable.'

'So she can't be far away, you think?'

'No, that's why it's such a dashed difficult thing to understand.'

'Could she be with a relative who's been

taken ill? Mother, father, sister or someone? Close friend?'

'Checked all those likelihoods, not a sign of her. I've even checked the hospitals and the doctor, nothing. Spent all morning on the telephone, checking. Nothing. Everything about the house says she's at home – but she's not. Gone. Vanished into thin air, so I thought I'd better report it.'

'Does the name Geoffrey Heddon mean anything to you?'

I had to ask the question. The fact that he had also vanished must have some bearing on the disappearance of Jean Naylor; such coincidences were invariably linked. Two people, a man and a woman who had both vanished at the same time from a little place like Aidensfield, must surely be connected. Although I had no wish to make unsupported allegations that the pair might be associating, there was no doubt the fact of their joint disappearance would rapidly circulate the village. My belief was that if I did not alert Mr Naylor, somebody else would.

'Heddon? No, Constable, can't say the name rings a bell. We haven't lived here very long and I'm away a lot; I don't know many of the locals. Might I ask why you are referring to him?'

'He's also disappeared, some time since half past ten last night. I've just heard from his wife, literally moments ago.'

Naylor's face blanched and he sat speechless for a few minutes, as if the possibility of his wife being unfaithful was something he'd never contemplated.

'I can't believe Jean would do that,' he whispered. 'I just cannot believe it.'

'I have to consider the possibility of a connection between them.' I lowered my voice.

'Of course you have, Constable, of course you have. But this is such a shock ... to think Jean might have another man, well, hell, I just cannot accept it. There must be some other explanation. What do you know about this man? Heddon, you said?'

I told him everything that I knew about Geoffrey Heddon and explained our procedures for dealing with such reports, reinforcing my statement that if a man and woman disappear together in such circumstances, it is not a matter for the police.

'So what can you do for me?' he asked, now very much subdued.

'I'll implement our "Missing from Home" procedures, Mr Naylor, but under the circumstances, we cannot organize a full-scale search, unless there is evidence she's in danger or the victim of a crime perhaps. In any case, I'll need a description.'

She was thirty-six years old, a tall, slim woman with auburn hair, good teeth, brown eyes and pierced ears. She always wore dangling ear-rings and, according to her husband, she'd be wearing jeans, sandals and a green T-shirt. All her other clothes were in her wardrobe – which, in his view, meant she had not run off with another man. As with Mrs Heddon, I asked Mr Naylor to supply me with a photograph of his wife as soon as possible, and assured him I would do my best to trace her even if, strictly speaking, it was not my duty.

I asked him to go home and wait near the telephone, but also to contact every known friend and relative in case she'd been called away urgently. When I rang Sergeant Craddock, I guessed his response – he said that if a man and woman choose to run away to start a new life together, it is not a matter for the police. If we did come across either or both of them, in the course of our general duties, we would notify the respective spouses of their safety, but we could not reveal their whereabouts. And so, in what would surely become a *cause célèbre* for

Aidensfield, I began that day's patrol around my large rural patch with a particular task in mind. I had a few other jobs too, including the delivery of a renewed firearm certificate to Malcolm Kelly at Thornton Farm.

During my patrol, I would ask at all likely places to see whether anyone had seen the couple, either individually or as a pair, or whether anyone knew if there was some kind of secret romance between them – it was the least I could do even if it was not really my responsibility. I decided I would complete my routine tasks first, I'd get them out of the way before concentrating on the missing pair, then I could give their absence my undivided attention. I knew that all our established procedures would already be in action, and I knew also that each of the remaining spouses would be doing everything within their power to track down their missing loved ones.

I decided my first call would be at Thornton Farm. I would deliver the certificate, then I had a couple of visits at Elsinby on behalf of Bradford Police, and a call at High Farm, Briggsby to check their stock register. I reckoned those few jobs would take less than an hour, and then I would return to Aidensfield to concentrate upon the village, asking for any sightings of Geoffrey Heddon and Jean Naylor. I drove my Mini-van slowly down the bumpy lane, past the isolated garage and on to Thornton Farm. I never gave the garage a thought – at this stage, I knew nothing of the circumstances which had led Malcolm to slam the door the previous night and, of course, it wasn't mentioned during my brief time at the farmhouse. On the return journey, however, I was chugging slowly up the rough track when I thought I glimpsed a movement at one of the windows. I wondered if a bird of some kind had become trapped inside and so I reduced my speed to gain a better and closer look at the tiny window. And I saw a human hand waving. I could not see into the garage, however, the window was too high for one thing and the morning sun was reflecting from it too, but I did see that movement. I stopped my van and went to the garage door. As I approached, I heard shouts.

'Hello, anybody there?' someone called faintly from within.

'Hello, yes, it's PC Rhea...'

'Oh, thank God,' cried a woman's voice. 'Thank God ... can you let us out?'

'I'll try,' I called back. 'If not, I can get the farmer to unlock it.'

I discovered the door was not locked from the outside. The large wooden sneck, extending almost the entire width of the doors in the manner of a medieval castle, held them firmly shut and no amount of thrusting from inside would have breached that security. It was the work of a moment to lift the sneck and pull open one of the doors and a weeping woman staggered out and collapsed on my shoulder.

She was sobbing with relief, crying, 'I thought we would die in there ... nobody came...'

'Some idiot slammed the door on us.' The man was doing his best to appear calm and unruffled by events. 'We couldn't get out, no way, and nobody came past. We shouted and shouted and hammered on the doors ... we've been there all night ... it was dreadful.'

He now took the woman in his arms and tried to comfort her as I said, 'Are you Geoffrey Heddon? And Jean Naylor?'

He nodded and now she looked at me with her eyes black with crying and her hair all awry. Then she nodded. At my reference to their names, she realized their plight was known to others.

'You've both been reported missing from home,' I told them. 'By your respective spouses. Separately, I might add. There's no hint you've been together. I'm going to radio my office now, to cancel our references. I will just say you have been traced and you are both fit and well. I think each of you had better inform your spouse, rather than me. You can deal with their questions.'

'But, I mean, what do I tell my wife?' blustered Heddon.

'And Paul, he'll never forgive me … oh, God, this is dreadful…'

'What you tell them is entirely up to you,' I told them. 'I'll not say where you were or how you were discovered. It means the ball's entirely in your own court! It's up to you to produce a convincing answer – or you could tell the truth! Now, can I give you a lift anywhere?'

'No,' said Heddon. 'I don't think so. I think we should walk; we need time to think about this, to come up with a plausible explanation … then I think we should approach the village from separate directions.'

I was about to say I would not mention the incident to Malcolm Kelly, the owner of the garage, when, almost on cue, he appeared behind us on his tractor. He saw the gathering of three at his garage and stopped, leaving the noisy engine running.

'Problems?' he asked from the high seat, turning his gaze to the door of his garage, now standing wide open.

'No, no problems. But did you close this garage door last night?' I asked, with a smile on my face.

'Aye, it was blowing in t'wind, I slammed it shut. Yon garage was empty, wasn't it?' he questioned, looking at the bedraggled couple at my side before realization dawned upon him.

I did not tell anyone about this episode, other than to inform Sergeant Craddock so that our files could be closed, but the story eventually surfaced in the village. I have no idea how the respective couple explained things to their spouses, but to their credit, neither Geoffrey Heddon nor Jean Naylor tried to blame Malcolm Kelly for their plight. That is totally unlike Cornelius and Carabella Hammond who blamed everyone else for their own mistakes.

One example was their picnic outing to Maddleskirk Forest. Since the 1930s, the Forestry Commission has nurtured several coniferous forests around the North York Moors and these occupy spectacular locations whilst giving sanctuary to a large variety of wildlife. Following the establishment of the national parks in 1952, and bearing in mind that the trees were then mature and so less prone to damage, it was decided to open some of the forest tracks to the public. Visitors would be encouraged, picnic areas would be created and car-parks installed – while ever-present fire risk would be hammered home to the tourists. By the time I became the village constable at Aidensfield, these forests had become highly popular with day-trippers and tourists – books were written about the area, viewing platforms and information centres were installed and new forest roads created. And so it was that Cornelius and Carabella decided to have a picnic in Maddleskirk Forest.

Cornelius was a little man, only some five feet tall and somewhat circular in appearance. He had a round face with round cheeks, and a very round head with scarcely a hair upon it. Even his rimless spectacles were round. Although he had a rounded body, he had a very straight back and broad shoulders which he held high, as if to emphasize his height – or lack of it. However he held himself, though, he always appeared more rounded than he wished, and he always looked too short for his circumference. In some respects, he was like a jenny wren, a dumpy little bird which can make a very loud noise. And Cornelius could make a very loud noise. If anyone heard Cornelius before catching sight of him, one might expect the arrival of a Collossus of some kind, not a tiny little chap with a bald head who strutted about his business with all the presence of a ruling monarch.

He and his wife had retired to Aidensfield after selling their thriving business. It was a clothes shop in Ashfordly, specializing in ladies and gentlemen's wear and in the window he'd placed a wonderful notice which proclaimed: 'Ladies and Gentlemen's alterations. 'This was always a source of humour, even if Cornelius could not understand the joke.

His wife, Carabella, thin and mouselike, was hardly any taller than Cornelius and, when in business, she had been keeper of the accounts, secretary, telephone answerer and general factotum. The business had been very successful, but Cornelius had one personality defect – he was extremely pompous. With his loud voice, he could quickly establish a presence among a crowd, even if most of them could not see him, and he commanded waiters, attendants, other shop assistants and anyone who was servile, to leap to his assistance – virtually upon pain of death for any slack or irreverent behaviour. I felt he could have had a wonderful career as a town crier.

And so it was, one lovely June morning, that he and Carabella packed their lunch and departed in their Ford Anglia for a picnic site in Maddleskirk Forest on the moors above Aidensfield. Upon arrival at the isolated site, they found they had the entire place to themselves which was just how Cornelius liked it, and so he parked his car close to one of the established picnic table-cum-benches and prepared to unpack his meal and picnic paraphernalia. It was in the boot, in a hamper, and so he and Carabella climbed out and went to the rear of the car. Carabella stood to one side as Cornelius displayed his strength by hoisting up the boot lid and heaving out the heavy hamper. But he had forgotten to secure the handbrake. As the car-park sloped slightly towards the picnic tables, the action of

Cornelius in opening the boot and lifting the hamper caused the car to move backwards. It ran into his body and he was not strong enough to halt its progress. Desperately, he leaned against it with all his weight, booming at Carabella to do something, but he failed and, as he tried to leap out of the way, he tripped over his own feet and fell to the ground, still clutching the hamper. Relentlessly but ever so slowly, the car rolled on and Cornelius found himself trapped beneath it. His legs disappeared under the rear axle and one wheel of the car came to rest against the hamper while the bumper touched the bench of the table. The car was securely parked now, it could not roll back any further but Cornelius was firmly trapped beneath it. He daren't struggle in case his movements caused the vehicle to resume its progress, but, in fact, the ground had a slight rise at that point and it would not roll any further. In his anguish, Cornelius was not to know that.

Apart from some burns from the exhaust, and a few bumps and bruises to his ample belly, he was not physically injured even if his huge pride was. The unfortunate thing was that Carabella could not drive and despite her husband's loud pleas and barked advice on how to set the handbrake, get into first gear and drive off, she would not touch the vehicle. She was terrified of causing serious injury to her husband if she moved it just one inch, and she said she would go for help.

It was perhaps unfortunate that the nearest farm was two miles away, something Carabella was unlikely to know until she set off, but when she reached the farm, the farmer, Reg Blenkinsop, rang the police, then called a garage with lifting gear and an ambulance in case Cornelius required hospital treatment. And he also drove Carabella back to her long-suffering husband who was still trapped under his car. When I arrived, he was still there, more than two hours later, but if his voice was anything to go by, he was not hurt – but he could not, or would not, risk moving. I applied the handbrake and talked to him as he lay with most of his rotund body beneath the vehicle, but it was clear he was not badly hurt. The ambulance arrived very soon after me, and we all decided it would be best to leave the vehicle as it was, and also not move Cornelius just yet. We did not want to risk further injury to him by our amateurish efforts. Eventually, a breakdown truck with lifting gear arrived at the scene and after inspection from all angles, we decided it could be hoisted high enough for Cornelius to be safely extracted. Very gently, the car was lifted at the rear end so that Cornelius could be hauled free, and then it was lowered gently to the ground once he was at a safe distance. It could now be driven away. In spite of his protests, Cornelius was placed in the ambulance because both I and the ambulance crew felt he should undergo a detailed examination in hospital. After this kind of experience, there could be hidden injuries, even if Cornelius loudly proclaimed otherwise. His wife was allowed to go with him in the ambulance. His car was locked and it would remain here for him to retrieve later.

From my point of view, this was not a reportable road traffic accident because the vehicle had not been on a public road at the time of the event. It was an incident, not an accident.

Cornelius was not detained in hospital because what injuries he did have were all very minor ones – superficial burns, scratches and bruises with no broken limbs or deep cuts – but I had to visit him at home to obtain a statement for our files. A few days later I called at his house and he settled me at his dining-room table which I could use as a desk, and as I led him through the series of events, it was clear it was all his fault – quite simply, he had failed to set his handbrake.

Had that occurred on a road, he would have committed an offence against the Motor Vehicles (Construction and Use) Regulations, but as this was on a car-park on private property, such a charge could not be levelled against him. In spite of his own lapse, Cornelius Hammond felt that his predicament had arisen through everyone's fault but his own.

'I'm going to sue the Forestry Commission,' he told me as I was about to leave his house.

'What on earth for?' I asked.

'For not having a level car-park,' he boomed.

There was another small mishap due to the actions of a man called Albert Deakin. Albert was a bit of a dreamer and after living and working in Rotherham for most of his life, doing muscle-aching labouring jobs in the steel industry, he yearned for retirement to a cottage on the moors. He sought something which was a complete contrast to his tough life in town – a life with no future other than a relentless slog. His wife, Marjorie, fully supported him in this dream – she was a poet who wrote unpublishable verses about birds in the sky. Because the couple escaped to the moors whenever they could, usually at weekends, their idea of heaven was to live a quiet life free from city smells, hard work, traffic and trades unions.

When the steel industry suffered under socialism, Albert lost his job long before he was due to retire, received some redundancy money and suddenly found himself heading for the moors on a house-hunting trip. And he found almost what he wanted – but not quite. It was a lonely dwelling high on the moors above Shelvingby, the former tied-cottage of a farm worker. High Rock Cottage was stone built with two bedrooms, a nice kitchen, lounge and dining room with a few outbuildings and a plot of land about quarter of an acre in size. The whole of the plot was surrounded by a dry-stone wall and the hill-top house commanded wonderful views across the moors. Although it had all the services, it needed some modernization, something Albert was more than capable of doing himself. He had enough money from his redundancy payment, the sale of his terraced house and his savings to pay for High Rock and to live for a few months until he found a way of earning his keep – he believed he could always get a job labouring on a farm, doing people's gardens, working in a garage, or even cleaning windows.

And so, in the June of that year, Albert and Marjorie moved into High Rock Cottage, Shelvingby to begin their rustic dream. I paid them a visit shortly after their arrival because Albert held a firearm certificate for a .22 BSA rifle and I needed to satisfy myself that all the details were correct so that it could be replaced with an updated one, issued by my own Force due to his new address. They invited me to join them for coffee. They seemed a lovely couple who were so delighted that their dream was almost a reality. For all Albert's sturdy toughness, I must admit I was rather surprised to find he was something of a dreamer. His practical side was already in evidence because he had transformed the kitchen, having done all the work himself, but I did get the impression that he was seeing life through those famous rose-coloured spectacles. It was during that visit that he and Marjorie told me High Rock Cottage lacked one part of their dream.

'So what's missing?' I smiled, as Marjorie brought me a coffee and chocolate biscuit – we were sitting outside on the patio that Albert had built, admiring the stunning views across the open moor from this lofty and lonely site. Marjorie was a quiet little woman whose hair was just turning grey – she'd be in her early fifties, I guessed, and wore round horn-rimmed specs on her round and pink face. Albert was taller and rather stooped with a lean appearance, but his iron-grey hair was thick and well tended, his clothes were dark and sombre and I noticed he wore heavy boots. A legacy of his working days perhaps?

'A stream,' said Marjorie. 'All I ever wanted was a cottage in the country with a stream at the bottom of the garden but I mustn't grumble. This cottage has everything else we ever wanted ... it's like heaven, Mr Rhea, it really is.'

'I might build a pond,' Albert said. 'There's plenty of room. It would attract wildlife, eh? And Marjorie could write her poems about the birds it attracts.'

I left them to their dream and they issued me with a standing invitation to pop in any time I was passing, but to be honest, High Rock Cottage was not the type of place anyone passed by – there had to be a deliberate intention to go there because it was rather off the proverbial beaten track with nothing beyond but countless square miles of heather-clad moorland. But it was charming, it was quiet, and it offered rustic bliss to those who could cope with the isolation and the ferocious conditions that prevailed each winter. Even High Rock Farm, to which it had once belonged, lay further down the dale.

The Deakinses' decision to buy High Rock Cottage coincided with a trend among many dreamy townspeople who were busily buying country cottages as weekend retreats. With many farms and country estates contracting and employing fewer people, they did not need so many tied houses, consequently hundreds of little cottages appeared on the market. Many were primitive and lacking modern amenities, but they fulfilled the needs of those who liked to get away from the smoke, grime, crime, traffic and bustle of towns in favour of what became known as a 'better quality of life'.

A lot of the buyers had no idea what they

were letting themselves in for, and few knew anything about country life and country ways but, as one of them said to me, 'I know I was born and bred in a town, but it was on the outskirts and there was a farm less than a mile away, so I do know something of country life.'

The result was that places like Shelvingby were swamped with townies who bought cottages and spent only a few days each year in the village, often wanting to change things to suit their needs. However, it also meant that cottages which might otherwise have become derelict were occupied and kept in a good state of repair. In addition, some cottagers did support the rural economy, if only by visiting the local pub – one or two shopped in the villages too, although most seemed to bring their own food and domestic necessities.

Such a couple were Sidney and Laura Compton who had a very successful contemporary furniture store in Leeds. In their mid-fifties, they had bought Ling Cottage on the moors above Shelvingby and were busy converting it to suit their expensive tastes. It was not quite so high or far on to the moor as High Rock Cottage and certainly not so remote, but it commanded nice views and was only a short walk away from the centre of the village. The moment anyone saw Sidney and Laura, they knew they were not rural folks – they were far too smartly dressed and always looked as if they were going to a wedding or a funeral. And their shoes were always clean!

Those who had visited Ling Cottage said it mirrored the appearance of its owners – it was beautifully furnished with the finest antiques surrounded by exquisite décor and the very latest in kitchen and bathroom furnishings. A little gem, in other words. And, like so many cottagers, the Comptons came only occasionally. They were far too busy to become yokels *every* weekend and in their absence, Ling Cottage was cared for by one of the village ladies. Mrs Armitage popped in once or twice a week to dust and clean, water the plants and do whatever chores were necessary.

Late in September, she had paid her usual Thursday morning visit to Ling Cottage, this time to dust the bedrooms, air the sheets and switch on the immersion heater to warm the water. She had also turned on the oil central heating to air the cottage because the Comptons had indicated they would be coning for the weekend, arriving late on Friday afternoon. As always, she had left the back door standing open while she worked and had also opened the front door to provide a through-draught as a means of airing the downstairs rooms and freshening the house. There was absolutely nothing unusual in her routine except that when she came downstairs after an hour or so, the ground floor was under four inches of water and the rockery in the back garden had been transformed into quite a spectacular waterfall.

A gush of water was flowing in through the back door, across the kitchen and into the front lounge, then out through the front door where it cascaded down the steps, flowed rapidly down the garden path and disappeared beneath the gate. There was a road beyond the gate, a steep hilly sort of road which would carry the flood away and, hopefully, into the stream which flowed at the foot of the village. That was the normal route for excess water which came off the moors, but there had been no heavy rain in recent weeks or days, and no melting snow.

Mrs Armitage, a countrywoman of many years' experience, was not the sort to flap or get into a dizzy state; she simply closed the back door and left the front one open, hoping that most of the water would drain away. In fact, most of it did – it moved nicely through the house and into the garden, albeit soaking carpets, furnishings, cupboards and floors *en route*. With its main point of entry now effectively blocked, the water simply flowed along the back of the house, found a way down the east side and into the garden; from there, it resumed its route down the front garden path and on to the road. A little of it continued to seep beneath the closed door, and, even with the main inlet closed, the house interior was left standing in an inch or so of water. Outside, there was a continuing threat because the floodwater was still flowing spectacularly down from the moors and over the rockery towards the back door, even if most of it was now diverted. It was not a modest trickle – it was like a moorland beck in full flow.

The phone was still working so Mrs Armitage rang the Comptons and then dashed down the village to the shop to see if anyone knew why the water had suddenly appeared and where it had come from. Furthermore, it must be stopped before it did more damage. Fortunately at this stage, it seemed to be affecting only the one cottage because it was flowing swiftly down the village street in a gutter which carried it down to the stream. That same gutter carried flood water along the same route and also water produced by melting snow.

By chance, I was on duty and in the village shop at the time and so I listened to Mrs Armitage's calm and simple tale.

'So where's it come from?' I asked.

'Nay, Mr Rhea, I've no idea. It's just started; it wasn't there when I let myself in, and then suddenly the house was awash.'

The shopkeeper, a man who'd lived in Shelvingby all his life, said, 'It sounds as if one of those gills up on the moor top has got blocked, even a dead sheep can block the flow and make the water rise over the banks. They're very narrow and it doesn't take much to make 'em flood or change direction. But if they do get blocked or change their routes, the water's only got one way to come – and that's down here. That's why we keep that gutter clear down the main street.'

'What's behind Ling Cottage?' I asked.

'There's nothing immediately behind,' the shopkeeper told me. 'Just the open moor, but if you keep heading north, you come to High Rock Farm, and beyond that there's nothing for miles, nothing but moor, that is.'

'High Rock?' I was alerted by the name. 'That's near High Rock Cottage?'

'Aye, not far off. Why?'

'I was at High Rock Cottage not long ago,' I told them. 'There's new folks there now, a couple from Rotherham. He was saying how he'd like a stream at the bottom of his garden! Look, I'll go up there right away,' I assured them. 'I want to see if he's been messing about with those gills on the moor.'

Albert Deakin had indeed been messing about with the gill behind his cottage.

On an exploratory walk one morning, he'd noticed a narrow strip of water winding its way through the heather and peat, and had realized it could easily be diverted towards his cottage, there to feed a stream through his garden. And it would fill his dream pond too...

And so he had diverted the water. He'd even excavated a pond at the bottom of his garden, lined it with clay and allowed the incoming water to fill it. In time, of course, it had overflowed – Albert had known it would do so and had calculated the excess water would find its way back to its original route. In fact, only that morning Albert had seen it working its way through the heather and, in his estimation, it had been heading towards the stream which flowed deep in the dale.

But the diverted water had had a mind of its own. It had not discovered its earlier route but had found a fast, easier and more direct path which had led it right through the middle of Ling Cottage.

Albert said he would speak to Mr and Mrs Compton and hoped they were insured, and added that he would re-divert the water.

My only comment about his action was that it was not a matter for the police.

Chapter Ten

During training courses for brand new constables at the time I joined the police service, recruits were not provided with much information about the art of detecting crime. That was considered the privilege of members of the elite Criminal Investigation Department who underwent their own specialized training. However, the initial course reminded us that MO (*modus operandi*) was an important ingredient of a crime, as was *mens rea* (the state of the criminal's mind), and we were also told that one method of finding the perpetrator, especially in a serious crime like murder, was to establish a motive. Quite often, that motive was obvious – revenge and greed were among the most prominent – but some motives were extremely devious and difficult to ascertain.

As a village constable, I was not called upon to solve many crimes although, as a police officer with responsibility for my own patch, I was expected to investigate a range of minor offences which might occur. Simple theft and malicious damage were two examples of the sort of crime I was expected to investigate without calling in the CID, but if a more serious case occurred, then the experts had to be summoned. Clearly, I would never be expected to deal alone with a murder enquiry or other serious crime like rape, burglary or robbery, but if such a crime did occur on my patch, then I might be co-opted to help in the investigation, particularly as I possessed a good deal of local knowledge. I must admit I enjoyed the challenge of crime investigation and whenever a crime occurred on my patch, I spent many hours trying to solve it. And I solved several.

Among my successes were two crimes for which the motives were extremely obscure. Perhaps 'crime' is too strong a word for the tales which follow, but in essence, these were criminal acts, albeit of a rather peculiar kind. The first incident involved Ashfordly Hospital.

When we patrolled during the night, attention to the local hospital or hospitals was always regarded as a key duty. At Ashfordly, there was just the one hospital – Ashfordly Cottage Hospital to give it its full name – and it served a wide area. Because the main doors were open twenty-four hours a day, and the receptionist was often a woman working alone, even at night, we made sure we paid regular visits in uniform to deter potential trouble-makers. The first hour or so after closing-time in the pubs, or after a dance turned out, was often a critical period with drunken yobs trying to gain entry, either to chat up the nurses, to visit friends in the wards, or just to be a nuisance. But we were also aware of more serious trespassers, such as those seeking drugs, those wishing to harm patients, or those intending to steal something from the hospital. For example, cloakrooms with toilets often sported coats belonging to hospital workers hanging on the walls and those coats often had cash or other valuables in the pockets. Hospital thieves knew where to look, and they also knew the hospital routine – and the value of wearing a white coat if they could find one! Those cloakrooms were easy sources of white coats, a ready and very simple disguise. Clearly, the police did their best to persuade the hospital staff not to leave white coats, or their own clothing, in such vulnerable locations. Some thieves would even tour the wards at night, dodging the ward sisters, and then stealing from the patients' bedside cabinets.

There were other peculiar characters known as hospital hoppers, people who pretended to be ill, often displaying the symptoms of a serious ailment. They would travel the country and turn up at a hospital to gain emergency admission by a session of skilful play-acting. Invariably they would provide a false name and an equally false medical history, and thus gain a few days in hospital with food, bedding and companionship. Some were even subjected to operations when the fact of their dishonesty would be discovered. Most hospitals – and the police – had lists of such people along with their MO. Some always claimed to have appendicitis, for example, others had breathing difficulties, or stomach problems – and all could create a wonderful impression of the genuine illness.

It follows that a police presence was always welcome by the hospital authorities – and we enjoyed these visits because it placed us, at least temporarily, in a warm environment if the night was wet or cold and it was also a good source of cups of tea, coffee and biscuits. And, of course, some of the nurses were angels in disguise.

Another source of trouble was nurses' homes. The nurses did not cause the problems – it was others who knew where they lived. There was such a place in the grounds of Ashfordly Hospital. It was nothing more than a modern brick-built block of one-bedroom flats with a common-room on the ground floor, a games-room, a television room, a laundry and a communal kitchen. Because nurses worked shifts around the clock, it meant the nurses' home was always busy with young ladies coming and going from the premises. There were no male nurses at that time.

The nurses did not have far to walk to get to their place of work, but at night the trek across the open ground between the home and the hospital did make them somewhat vulnerable, especially if they were walking alone. Although physical or sexual attacks on nurses were rare, they could and did happen sometimes, more frequently in the larger urban areas than in Ashfordly. Nurses' homes also attracted peepers, or peeping toms. Far more common than attacks on nurses they were just as frighten-ing, even if these sad people wanted nothing more than the sight of a pretty young woman in her underwear or without any clothing at all. One of our regular chores was to ask the hospital authorities to speak to the residents of these homes and plead with them to close their curtains, especially at night or when dressing, undressing or having a bath. A gap in a curtain at night, with the light shining through, is like a magnet to peeping toms, especially in a ground-floor room or one which can be viewed easily from a high point such as a fire escape, wall top or even a tree!

They are attracted by the slim slivers of light which appear from carelessly drawn curtains just as a moth heads for a bright light and the peepers then press their faces against the available windows to catch a glimpse of exposed female flesh. Often the unfortunate girl would notice the face, scream for all she was worth and cause an almighty fuss during which the culprit would escape in the darkness.

Some did not attempt to get very close to their victims – they viewed from afar, finding gaps in curtains and then, with binoculars on occasions, watching for the unclothed occupants.

Catching a peeping tom was a rare occurrence – if we placed a police officer in the grounds, you could be sure he would be spotted first by the peeper who would then fade into the darkness. An added danger was that the earnest young constable might himself be mistaken for a peeper by a nurse or even a nurse's boyfriend.

The name Peeping Tom comes from the story of Lady Godiva. Godiva was the wife of Leofric, the Earl of Mercia who died in 1057. Leofric had imposed punitive taxes on his tenants and Godiva tried to persuade her husband to remove them. Somewhat rashly, he promised to remove the taxes if she would ride naked through the streets and she did so, her modesty protected only by her long hair. The earl kept his promise. However, everyone in the town knew in advance of Godiva's plan and when the time came for the ride, all the citizens remained indoors as a mark of respect and to prevent embarrassment to Godiva. But one man could not contain his interest – he was a tailor called Tom and, as Lady Godiva rode past, he peered through a gap in the curtains to catch sight of her. He was struck blind at that moment and has since been known as Peeping Tom.

Peeping is not a specific crime in this country, but if an offender is caught, he (or she) is taken to court to be bound over to be of good behaviour, or to keep the peace, or to abstain from further incidents of like kind. This kind of behaviour is regarded as a common law nuisance and as such it can be dealt with in the courts even if it does not feature in any written statute. Somewhat surprisingly, the wonderful system of binding over people to be of good behaviour, or to keep the peace, was established by the Justice of the Peace Act of 1361 – it is now almost 650 years old and no better system for dealing with such matters has yet been devised. Usually, a period of time is specified in the Binding Over order, perhaps two or three years, and if the person reoffends in that time, he or she can be punished for the original matter, as well as any additional offence. If this is accompanied by a splash of local publicity with an account of exactly what the perpetrator was doing, it usually prevents further incidents, at least for a short time. We made sure the local newspaper knew when such a case was to be heard in the local court!

And so it was, against this background, that we began to receive reports of a peeping tom in the grounds of Ashfordly Cottage Hospital, especially in the vicinity of the nurses' home. I was told of the problem as I paraded for night duty at Ashfordly Police Station one damp and misty September evening. We'd had a week or so of dense mists and chilly weather, and it was my turn to perform a week of night shifts in the GP car. This vehicle, the General Purpose car, patrolled the entire division overnight, dealing with any urgent matter that might arise, but also paying attention to routine matters like dance halls, clubs and pubs turning out their regulars, the supervision of explosive stores at quarries, the checking of vulnerable premises, monitoring the movements of known villains and so forth.

At ten o'clock that night, as I examined the Occurrence Book for details of stolen vehicles, wanted persons and recorded crimes, Sergeant Craddock appeared from his office.

'Glad I caught you before you vanish into the great unknown, PC Rhea,' he beamed. 'I've a nice little night-time duty for you this week.'

'I'm all ears!'

'We've had a call from the hospital, a prowler has been spotted in the grounds, hanging about the nurses' home,' he said. 'Usual thing, I suppose, a peeper, some sad case wanting to see the nurses in the all-together.'

'I'll call in,' I said. 'I'll park the car in the grounds too, it'll display a police presence which should help deter the peeper. Have we more details of him?'

'No, not a lot. PC Ventress went to see the nurse who reported the original sighting and all she could say was that she spotted a dark, shadowy figure standing under a tree near the path that leads from the hospital to the home. It was just after ten o'clock as she was coming off shift, and very dark. When she shone her torch at him, he ran off, but she didn't recongize him and can't provide a description. She ran inside and told one of the sisters who was watching television, and they both looked around outside but saw nothing. The sister reported it to the matron who told the registrar. The peeper was seen again a week later – that was last night in fact – standing in the same place, and again ran off when he was noticed.'

'Not a lot to go on,' I said.

'No, the thing will be to catch him in action, that might mean hiding in the grounds if he becomes more of a nuisance, or more persistent. He can't get into the nurses' home, by the way, all the doors are kept locked and the residents have their own keys. The nurses have been told to close their curtains at night.'

'That usually does the trick!' I smiled. 'Keeps the moths from being attracted!'

'I know there's not a lot we can do about these peepers but there you are, a troublesome matter for you to consider during your rounds.'

'I'll pop into the hospital tonight, Sergeant, and see what I can learn about it; there's bound to be gossip among the nurses. It wouldn't surprise me if others have noticed him but not reported it.'

As some of the nurses changed shifts at ten o'clock, and it was ten while I was being briefed by Sergeant Craddock, I had missed that evening's danger period. However, as the hospital was literally just a minute's drive from the police station, my first action was to get there as quickly as I could, just in case the peeper was active. I parked prominently outside the main entrance and made my presence known to the night receptionist who directed me to the night sister. I found her at her desk. She had supervised the change of shifts and was now checking her patients' records in readiness for the coming night. I had no wish to disrupt her work nor, at this early stage of my patrol, to avail myself of a cup of coffee, but she smiled and said, 'Can I help, Constable?'

'I'm announcing my presence, that's all,' I assured her. 'We've had reports of a peeper in the grounds and I thought I'd have a wander around, show the uniform and so on. I wanted you to know, just in case you get more reports – tonight, it'll be me pottering about in the darkness, not a prowler. I'll let you know when I leave.'

'Thanks, it's made some of our nurses a bit nervous. Most of them go in twos or threes from here at night, but every so often, a nurse finds herself having to cross the grounds alone. It can be a bit nerve-racking, knowing there's a weird character hanging about.'

'So how often has he been seen? Would you know?'

'It's difficult to say. I don't see all the nurses, due to their shifts, but according to the tales circulating the hospital, he's been spotted once or twice during the past week, and again last night. Just standing under that tree near the boundary wall. He's not approached any of the girls and has run off the minute he realizes he's been spotted.

They've been told not to tackle him but to ignore him as best they can, and inform the hospital staff. We'll then decide whether or not to involve the police, that's the usual procedure.'

'Good advice. I'd like to add that it would be helpful if we could get some kind of description of him – age, height, colour of hair, the clothing he wears, unusual features, anything helpful, with as much detail as possible.'

'I'll do what I can,' she promised. 'I'll leave a note for Matron.'

And so I left for a patrol around the grounds.

I did not try to conceal myself on this occasion, I wanted the prowler, if he was lurking in the darkness, to realise that we knew about his activities. So I walked around the grounds flashing my torch and directing its beam into all the likely hiding places. A lone nurse did cross from the hospital to the home while I was there. She made use of the concrete path across the grass and I made myself known to her. I walked with her, flashing my torch from side to side as we walked, but she said she'd not seen the prowler, nor had she had any frightening experiences in the grounds at night and tended to regard the affair as some kind of joke. She maintained she wasn't in the least perturbed by a sad man watching her from a distance, so long as that's all he did – after all, she was accustomed to dealing with all manner of odd characters on the wards. I watched her unlock the door and vanish into the interior of the nurses' home. I knew that word of my presence would now circulate among the nurses. Although I remained on the premises for almost an hour, spending some time under the tree which had sheltered the peeper, I saw nothing suspicious and wondered if my presence had been a deterrent. I bade farewell to the night sister, assured her I would look in again tomorrow night and continued my patrol around the remainder of the division.

I repeated those actions every night during that week of patrols and although I did not catch sight of any prowlers, I learnt, from my visits to the hospital itself, that rumours of the peeper had become very rife and persistent. Most certainly, the resident nurses took it very seriously indeed and if nothing else had been achieved, they were locking their doors and closing their curtains at night.

Then, on my final night duty for that session, a Sunday, I revisited the hospital and this time found a nurse sitting with the night sister – Sister Aldridge – and looking distraught.

'This is Nurse Briggs,' the sister introduced me. 'I said you'd be calling in about now and thought she'd better talk to you.'

The nurse was not a young woman. I estimated she would be in her mid-thirties, a thick-set person with heavy thick-lensed spectacles, fair hair showing beneath her uniform cap and a rather pale, rather flabby, complexion.

'I'm PC Rhea,' I introduced myself to her. 'So, Nurse Briggs, what's happened?'

'He was out there again, under that tree,' and she sniffed as she wiped her nose and eyes. 'Just standing there as I was going home.'

'How long ago?' I interrupted – if it was only a matter of minutes, he could still be out there. I might just find him.

'When I went off duty at ten o'clock,' she sniffed.

It was almost half past ten now, but I asked the two women to remain in the ward office while I rushed outside to make a search. Armed with my torch, I circled the hospital, checked the surroundings of the nurses' home, looked in the cars parked in the staff area, shone my torch through the thin mist into clumps of rose bushes, rhododendrons and assorted shrubs, but found nothing and no one. Finally, I decided to check beneath the tree where he'd been seen – it was a small sycamore, the only tree overlooking the path between the home and the hospital.

I thought there might be footprints in the soft earth – but instead I found a pile of cigarette butts and lots of dry, dusty ash. I had not noticed any of these during my earlier visits but saw they were all Benson and Hedges Silk Cut with filter tips, smoked only to half their length. I counted them – there were thirty – and I retrieved just one which I slipped into my pocket as a possible item of evidence. It seemed that the culprit stood beneath this tree and puffed cigarettes while watching the nurses.

If a man stood in the darkness smoking a cigarette, the burning end was often a give-away. The tiny red glow could readily be seen in the dark and the smell of the smoke on the night air could also reveal a smoker's presence. At this stage, I was undecided whether or not to mention this to the women – I did not want my knowledge of those clues to inadvertently reach the suspect at this early stage. I would decide how relevant it was. All I had to do now was to find a man who smokes Benson and Hedges Silk Cut with filter tips! I thought he must have been there a long time to get through all those cigarettes – or get halfway through them all – but as I'd not noticed any such cigarette ends on previous visits, felt that these confirmed his presence. If he'd chain-smoked all these during a single visit, he must have been standing there for an hour or more, waiting and watching. I felt they were the outcome of just one visit because the butts were all dry – had they lain on the ground for any length of time in these misty conditions, they would have been damp.

I wondered if the peeper had spent time waiting for a nurse to walk, along the path, observed her enter the nurses' home and then learned which was her room because he would see the light switched on. If it was on the ground floor, or within sight of some vantage point within the grounds with a gap in the curtains, he might then attempt his peeping activities.

I returned to the hospital for a further chat

with Nurse Briggs. Now that she had had time to calm down a little, I wondered if she could provide any sort of description of the peeper. When I got back she was in control of herself and was sipping a mug of tea with Sister Aldridge. I was invited to join them as the other ward nurses went about their business in their usual quiet and efficient manner.

'No sign of him,' I said. 'I think, we've scared him off. Now, Nurse Briggs, what can you tell me about him? I need a description if you can give one.'

'I can't really say what he looked like.' She shook her head. 'It was just a dark figure under the tree, tall I think, but I can't say what he looked like.'

'Did he say anything?'

'No, nothing. When I saw him standing there I just ran, I ran back, here. I didn't want him chasing me and me having to unlock the doors ... I panicked, I think, but it was awful.'

'You said he was there again? Have you seen him before?'

'Yes,' she said. 'About a week ago. I was coming off this shift and he was there. I'd not seen him before, Mr Rhea, and so I reported it to Matron like we have to, but I can't say what he looks like.'

'I thought he was a tall man?'

'Yes, I'd say so. Quite tall, but he could be young or old, black or white... I just don't know.'

'Well, if he does try to do anything stupid, make as much noise as you can and run as fast as you can, here into the hospital where there's people around. We'll pay attention during the week – it won't be me next week because I change shifts, but I'll tell my colleagues and they'll keep an eye on things for as long as necessary.

'Thank you,' she said. 'I hope you don't think I'm being silly...'

'Not at all,' I assured her. 'We need to know about this sort of thing. We can't stop it if we don't know it's happening. So, thanks for alerting us. Now, shall I escort you home?'

'Oh.' She brightened up considerably. 'Oh, yes, that is kind of you ... thank you so much.'

When she left the cover of the desk, I saw she was a short, dumpy woman with very heavy legs and a kind of waddling walk; she looked much older than I had first thought. However, she walked at my side as I led her out of the hospital and along the concrete path. I glanced at the sycamore but there was no sign of anyone lurking in its shadows and so I waited as she unlocked the main door of the nurses' home and vanished inside, with a very loud, 'Goodnight and thank you' to me. I thought the entire complex would hear her!

I did not resume my patrols. Instead, I returned to the hospital and sought Sister Aldridge once more. She was surprised to see me, but when I said I'd like a word in confidence, she took me into a small office and closed the door.

'What is it?' There was a slight look of apprehension on her face.

'What can you tell me about Nurse Briggs?' I asked.

She looked at me steadily for a few moments, as if trying to understand the purpose of my question, and then said, 'She's a very good nurse, Mr Rhea. I have no qualms about leaving her in charge of a patient. We work together from time to time, not this week though, but our shifts coincide on occasion.'

'I was thinking more along the lines of her personal life,' I said, lowering my voice.

'Are you thinking what I am thinking?' She smiled knowingly.

'That she's making up the story of the prowler?' I said.

'Why would she do that?' challenged the sister.

'To gain attention, sympathy, a few moments of fame … anything,' I replied.

'So what makes you think she's making it all up?'

'She told me she'd seen the man under the sycamore tree near the footpath and when I looked there tonight, I found thirty cigarette ends, all half smoked. That's more than a packet – if he'd smoked a packet of twenty while waiting there, he'd have been there a mighty long time. He might have discarded the packet too, but there was no packet. And the ash was concentrated around the butts. It was dry, not dampened by the mist. If they'd been there more than a few hours, all those butts would have been damp. If a man had stood there smoking, the ash would have wafted away. I believe those cigarette ends were planted there, Sister, taken from the hospital perhaps, an ash-tray emptied into a bag and the contents then dumped under that tree, to give credence to the story of the prowler.'

'A neat theory,' she smiled. 'And might I ask what kind of cigarettes they were?'

'Benson and Hedges,' I said. 'Filter-tipped. Who smokes those, I wonder?'

'Not your average Players or Woodbines?' she smiled. 'We do have a patient who chain-smokes Benson and Hedges with filter tips. Mr Shepherd in ward eight.'

'Does he smoke in the ward?'

'No, if he wants a smoke he has to go to the rest room. He spends a lot of time in there,' she smiled. 'Lost behind a haze of smoke.'

'So it would be easy for Nurse Briggs to pop in there, empty his ash-tray into a bag of some sort and remove the butts?'

'Very easy, especially towards the end of her late shift.'

'And what about Mr Shepherd? Is he likely to have nipped outside for a smoke and spent time under that tree? A long time by the look of things.'

She laughed. 'No, he's in a wheelchair; he has no legs. He lost them in the war, so he could never be described as a man standing under a tree! Those cigarettes could not have been dropped there by Mr Shepherd, I'm sure of that. And no one else smokes Benson and Hedges, not even members of staff.'

'Thanks. So back to my original question.

What do you know about Nurse Briggs?'

The sister sighed. 'She is not too popular with the other girls, Mr Rhea. They go off to the cinema, or to a club, or out for a drink either with some boyfriends or as a group, and she's never invited. It's sad really, she never does them any harm. She has no family either, no parents or brothers or sisters. She spends her off-duty time in the nurses' home, Mr Rhea, reading by herself or watching television. It's a lonely life.'

'She's not as young as the others, I would guess?'

'No, she's been a nurse a long time; she's in her mid thirties now, late thirties even. I think the younger ones think she's too old for a night out! For a twenty-year-old trainee, Briggs looks like a mother figure. I think she's aware of that.'

'I know how she feels! Now I must ask this: has she shown other signs of drawing attention to herself?'

'Yes, on several occasions. The senior staff here are aware of it and generally take very little notice. In fact, I think the nurses know about her tendencies too. To my knowledge, she once reported a black dog roaming the hospital and we had a huge search but found nothing. Then she said a man had followed her in town when she was shopping and on another occasion she reckoned she had spotted a wanted man in Ashfordly, she'd seen his photograph on a poster outside the police station. That was in Sergeant Blaketon's time. And now she's reported a prowler in the grounds...'

'I think you've said enough.' I thanked her. 'I'll leave things tonight, but next week, when I'm back on day duties, I'll call and have a word with her. I'll remind her that people who make a nuisance of themselves are liable to be bound over to be of good behaviour.'

'But suppose it is true, Mr Rhea? Suppose she is telling the truth? That's something we can't ignore, which is why we told the police.'

'We can't ignore these reports either. The only way to prove she's telling the truth is to catch the peeper and get him bound over,' I smiled. 'But I have a sneaking suspicion that a timely word with Nurse Briggs will bring an end to this little matter.'

I did speak to Nurse Briggs later that week and explained my theory about the appearance of the cigarette butts, but she persisted in her claim that she had seen a man loitering under that tree. Perhaps she had, perhaps it was a friend of one of the other nurses, but we received no more complaints about that peeping tom.

And her motive in making what seemed to be false claims? We never knew, except it might have been some kind of cry for help or a means of getting someone to show interest in her.

The other case involved a railway line. I arrived in Aidensfield shortly after the Beeching Report was published. That was in 1963 – I arrived in 1964. The outcome of this report is well known – Beeching's famous axe closed lots of railway lines throughout the country, especially some smaller branch lines in rural areas.

The line which served Aidensfield was still open when I arrived as the village constable. From Harrowby where it linked with the main line to York and London, it ran through the dale to Elsinby and along the valley towards Ploatby Junction where one branch turned away to serve Ashfordly, Brantsford and beyond to Scarborough while the other headed for Malton. It was not widely used but the occasional freight train would chug along its picturesque route, and four times a day, a passenger train would also make its way along the valley, two trips each weekday morning (one up and one down) and two each afternoon (one up and one down). In addition, there were sometimes extra trains, usually those hired for a special occasion or to accommodate day trippers, and these often appeared at weekends.

In rural areas, people often used the side of their local railway track as a footpath because it was level and formed the most direct route between two villages. Indeed, when I was a child I walked two miles to school and two miles back again every school day, invariably along my local railway line because it was shorter and perhaps safer than walking by road. And the station masters, porters and railway staff, including the engine drivers and guards, knew that children were regularly using the side of the track as a footpath. There was never any injury or incident involving children. They knew when a train was likely to arrive, and the drivers knew that children would be on the lineside before and after school. It was a far cry from life in the late twentieth and early twenty-first centuries, when this kind of relaxed attitude could never be permitted. To allow children on the tracks today can never be sanctioned, no matter how quiet the line. But in some rural areas, change is slow to make an appearance.

It was no surprise to me, therefore, to learn that primary school children walked regularly along the line between Ploatby to Elsinby, to attend the village school in Elsinby. For them, it was by far the shortest and most direct route. Three families of children made use of this facility – the Forresters comprised three youngsters, the Carrs were a family of four and the Bottomleys had only two, but it meant that a small party of nine children, a mixture of boys and girls all under nine years of age, made the daily trip in term time. Sometimes they walked as a group of nine, and sometimes they straggled along in smaller units, not necessarily of family members only. For most of the time, they used the track at around the same time of day – before nine on a school morning, and again after three-thirty in the afternoon.

From time to time, I chatted to the man who staffed the signalbox at Elsinby Station, and although I expressed some reservation about this route, he assured me the youngsters had never given cause for complaint or worry – for them, their daily trek was the most natural thing in the world, just like other children taking the bus to school, or walking or riding their bikes along the road, and the authorities were aware of the practice.

Then I received a complaint. Around 10.30 one morning, the signalman at Elsinby, Sid Garbutt, rang me and asked if I could pop in for a word with him. At that point, he did not give a reason and I said I would be there within the hour. I mounted the short wooden staircase up to his signal-box, a wonderful structure of wood with huge windows and brass fittings every-where, along with a row of massive handles by which he changed the points and oper-ated the signals. It was always warm in that signal box, especially in winter when his coke-burning stove threw out masses of heat and in summer when the windows pro-duced a greenhouse effect.

'Morning, Sid,' I greeted him. 'Trouble, is it?'

'Hello, Mr Rhea, sorry to drag you into this, but I didn't want to ring York and get the railway police all the way out here. They make such a fuss about things and, for this, I thought we could sort it out locally.'

'Seems sensible to me. So what's happened?'

'The platelayers found two sleepers across the track this morning. They'd been placed there deliberately. If a train had hit them, it could have been derailed. Luckily, the platelayers found them before a train came past and put them aside.'

'Children, you mean?' I asked, knowing the thoughts that were going through his mind.

'It's the sort of thing they do. They don't appreciate the danger; it's just a bit of fun in their eyes which is why I wanted it sorted out locally, without a fuss. A word with the school maybe, or with their parents. That's all that's needed.'

'Leave it with me,' I said. 'I'll speak to the headmistress this morning. So what time did it happen?'

'They were found after the first train had gone through, that's the down train to Malton. It comes through here at eight twenty-five each weekday morning. The platelayers found the sleepers about ten past nine. That's quite a while before the next train is due – the up train comes through at twenty past eleven.'

'And whereabouts were the sleepers?' was my next question.

'About two hundred yards this side of Hollin Bridge,' he said. 'Two sleepers on the track – it's a single track there as you might know.'

'So where would they get the sleepers from?'

'There are piles of them along the lineside,' Sid told me. 'They're old ones which have been replaced. When the sleepers are renewed, the old ones are put aside and the idea is to sell them for kindling or for making posts or even steps – they've a wonderful range of purposes – but they tend to get forgotten. These were replaced about six years ago. They're good solid chunks of wood, well creosoted and ideal for firewood. They're big objects, Mr Rhea, eight foot or so long by eight inches deep and fifteen inches wide, give or take a bit here and there. Solid bits of wood.'

'And the platelayers? They do a regular run along the track, I believe, checking the lines and points, tapping in the chocks. If my knowledge is correct, they start their day at Ploatby Junction and use that little bogey to trek all the way to Harrowby and back again?'

'Right, they time things so that the bogey's on a siding or double line when a train comes through.'

'Right, thanks, Sid. If it happens again, let me know. I'm sure we can sort this out without the York Railway Police getting involved. Leave it with me, and I'll let you know what happens.'

'Thanks, Mr Rhea.'

I knew the children concerned.

After spotting them making this daily trek soon after my arrival as the local constable, I had queried the practice with the headmistress of Elsinby School and with the local railway authorities and had then received all the assurances I needed. After all, I could understand – I'd done, in fact, exactly the same thing when I was attending primary school. As I walked towards the school, however, I began to ponder the situation. There'd been no previous incidents of this kind and although it was the sort of thing a child would do, I wondered if this group of youngsters, all very small children, were capable of lifting heavy sleepers and placing them across the lines. Individually, they most certainly could not lift one but collectively? Or a group of two or three? Even then I doubted it. Teenagers would be capable of doing so but children under eight or nine? Furthermore, the platelayers on their little bogey virtually followed the children along the line so would the bairns risk a trick like this knowing that officials were very close behind?

By the time I arrived at the school, I decided that I would not overtly blame those three families of children. I decided to treat them as witnesses rather than suspects. After explaining the situation to the headmistress, Miss Alice Snowdon, and expressing my doubts that any of her children were the culprits, she allowed me to address the children. There was only about forty of them and they all went into the big room to listen to me – talking to children was a regular part of my duties.

I began by saying, 'I just want to tell you not to play on the railway lines. You won't do this, will you?'

'No, sir,' came a chorus of little voices accompanied by much shaking of heads.

'And you won't go on to the railway lines, will you?'

'No sir,' they all chanted sing-song-like with more shaking of heads.

'Did any of you go on the railway lines this morning?' I put to them.

As most of the group chanted 'No sir,' nine hands shot up. 'Please, sir, we did,' said a very alert member of the Forrester family. She was Emily, aged nine. 'We walk to school by the line. Me and Rebecca and Rosie and Alan and John and Elizabeth and Mary and Andrew and Fiona.'

'And what did you do on the lines?' I asked.

'Nothing, sir, just walked to school like our mum says we must. She says we haven't time to play about and go bird nesting or playing hide and seek so we just walk fast all the way, to get here before the bell rings for assembly.'

'And did you see anybody on the line?'

'Just the train, sir, we hear it coming and get into the side.'

'Mr Henderson says we must not walk on the line,' piped up one of the little boys. 'So we keep the side, but he always says we must not walk on the line.'

'Mr Henderson?' I asked, not recognizing the name.

Miss Snowdon enlightened me. 'He's a retired railway official from York,' she explained. 'He bought that old railway-worker's cottage between here and Ploatby.'

'I don't know it,' I had to admit. Walking down railway tracks was not part of my duty.

'It's on the lineside,' she said. 'Not far from Hollin Bridge. They put it on the market about a year ago and Mr Henderson moved in recently. He's a railway fanatic, he admits that, which is why he bought the cottage. He just loves to be near trains.'

'Ah.' Now I understood, and so I redirected my attention to the children.

'Did you see Mr Henderson this morning?'

'He was standing in his garden and shouted at us not to walk on the line,' said Emily.

'And what did you do?'

'Nothing, sir, we just kept walking, not on the line, on the side of the track like Mum says we must.'

I did not want to ask them if they'd placed any kind of obstruction on the track because if they hadn't, it might plant dangerous ideas in their heads, but after talking to them about their daily walk to school, I could not honestly believe they had misused those railside sleepers. I decided I must talk to Mr Henderson. Perhaps he'd seen someone trespassing or misbehaving? After repeating my warning to the children not to play on the lines and thanking Miss Snowdon for allowing me that short time with them, I left. A quick examination of my local map showed that a road led to the railway cottage along the track; in fact, the lane passed over the railway at Hollin Bridge. And that's where the sleepers had been found this morning. I parked on the lane and walked the few yards to Railway Cottage, the name being on the gate.

As I walked towards the gate I could hear a petrol-driven lawnmower operating and found my way into the front garden where I discovered a slender, tall, grey-haired man at work. He spotted me, peered at me over his spectacles, then switched off his machine. I saw that the garden was full of railway artefacts – I spotted a signal, a bench bearing the name Elsinby, a former goods van which now served as a garden hut, a lamp post of the kind you'd find on a railway platform and some brass oil lamps in the windows of his cottage.

'Good morning, Constable.' He wiped his hands on a piece of rag. 'What can I do for you?'

'Mr Henderson?' I asked.

'Yes.' It was not a warm welcome, not the sort one expects in the countryside, and my first instinct was that this man was on the defensive.

'I believe you warned a group of children about walking on the line,' I began. 'This morning, it would be. And perhaps at other times?'

'Indeed I did!' he snorted. 'Little devils … they're trespassing, Constable, it is an offence against the railway regulations, and apart from that, it is dangerous. You can't have children on the lines without an element of danger. I should know, I have spent my whole life on the railways, both at work and as a hobby, and I have repeatedly warned them not to walk on the line but they ignore me, Constable, those Ploatby children defy me.'

'They have been walking along this line to school for as long as it has been here, Mr Henderson, without incident or complaint, and with the knowledge of the authorities, I might add.'

'That does not alter the situation. It is illegal, Constable, and you must do your duty.'

'When you say they should not walk along the line, they take you literally, they keep off the metals and walk along the side, not on the actual tracks.'

'You're splitting hairs, Constable! You know very well what I mean.'

'Yes, I do, but these are children, they take things literally.'

'Well, all I want is to have them stopped. It is an offence and if you are the local constable, you should prosecute them.'

'They are too young to be prosecuted, Mr Henderson, they are all under ten, that's below the age of criminal responsibility.'

'It is dangerous, Constable, that is what is important. It is against the regulations and it is dangerous, which is why I insist you should stop them.'

'It is not dangerous, Mr Henderson. There has never been a reported incident of any kind and no child has been injured. I do not feel justified in stopping a local practice that has been going on for years and years without incident.'

'So what about those sleepers on the track? Obstructing the line … if that's not dangerous, I don't know what is!'

'What sleepers?' I asked, awaiting his answer.

I could see the look of desperation which had crept into his eyes and at that moment I knew who had placed those sleepers on the track … they had been placed at a time and in a place where he knew the platelayers would find them before they were struck by a train. A child would never have considered things in that way.

'Tell me about the sleepers, Mr Henderson.

'I don't know anything about any sleepers, Constable. It was a figure of speech, the sort of tricks children get up to–'

'How did you know sleepers had been placed on the track, Mr Henderson?' I pressed him for an answer.

'That's why you are here, isn't it? To enquire about them?'

'How did you know they were there, Mr Henderson?' I repeated.

'Well, I went for a walk...'

'Not along the track, surely?' I interrupted. 'I thought that was illegal?'

'I saw them on the line.'

'But didn't remove them, eh? You left them for the platelayers to find and remove. Not a very responsible act, if I may say so ... can I suggest, just between the two of us, that you might have placed them there, Mr Henderson, as a devious means of getting the children into trouble, to get them stopped from using the line?'

'You can suggest what you like, Constable!' he snapped. 'I shall never admit to doing anything to put trains at risk! But if you won't do anything, then I shall report those children to the authorities in York. I will have them prevented from walking along this track!' And he turned to walk away from me.

'One thing before you leave, Mr Henderson. Those items of railway property in your garden, this seat, the signal, those lovely lamps in your windows … where did you get them? Aren't they all items of railway property?'

He stopped and sighed. 'You don't want me to stop those children, do you?'

'I don't think you will now, will you, Mr Henderson?'

I was never sure of Henderson's deeper motives in trying to get a party of very young children blamed for something they had not done, but I wondered if he felt the line beyond his garden was part of his retirement plot. I don't think safety of the children was uppermost in his mind. I think he wanted that line all to himself, to become his own private world. But that never happened. When the line was closed by Beeching's axe, the rails and sleepers were removed and it was used as a public footpath. Henderson didn't welcome the intrusion; he sold his house and bought a terraced cottage overlooking the main line in York. From there, he could watch the trains in peace. And the children of Ploatby still use the former track to walk to their primary school in Elsinby.

The publishers hope that this book has given you enjoyable reading. Large Print Books are especially designed to be as easy to see and hold as possible. If you wish a complete list of our books please ask at your local library or write directly to:

Magna Large Print Books
Magna House, Long Preston,
Skipton, North Yorkshire.
BD23 4ND

This Large Print Book, for people
who cannot read normal print,
is published under the auspices of

THE ULVERSCROFT FOUNDATION